P9-BYZ-771

Books by Linda Winstead Jones

LINDA WINSTEAD JONES

has written more than fifty romance books in several subgenres: historical, fairy tale, paranormal, and of course romantic suspense. She's won the Colorado Romance Writers Award of Excellence twice, is a three time RITA® Award finalist and (writing as Linda Fallon) was winner of the 2004 RITA® Award for paranormal romance.

Linda lives in North Alabama with her husband of thirty-four years. She can be reached via www.eharlequin.com or her own Web site, www.lindawinsteadjones.com.

LINDA WINSTEAD JONES

The Guardian

Silhouette®

Romantic

SUSPENSE

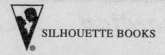

SILHOUETTE BOOKS

ISBN-13: 978-0-373-27582-3
ISBN-10:   0-373-27582-X

THE GUARDIAN

Visit Silhouette Books at www.eHarlequin.com

Printed in U.S.A.

"I'm not going to stay," Dante said bluntly. He wouldn't be less than honest with her.

"I know," Sara whispered.

"I'm not going to change my life or who I am, not for you or anyone else."

"I wouldn't ask you to."

"We're just two unattached adults looking for a little fun. That's it."

"If you say so." She grabbed his belt with one hand and held on.

"Nothing is going to—"

Sara interrupted him with a laugh. "Dammit, Dante, why don't you just shut up and kiss me?"

Dear Reader,

In many ways, it's easier to write about a character who's appeared in a couple of previous stories. You already know him and can avoid the sometimes lengthy process of discovering those wonderful and annoying traits that make him unique.

But I have discovered a flip side. Dante Mangino has been a favorite character of mine for years now. He's made an appearance in several other stories that featured investigators from the Benning Agency. But after his secondary story line in *One Major Distraction,* I had a very difficult time finding a woman for him. Maybe he was still grieving for the love he lost, or maybe I simply couldn't find a woman worthy of him. In any case, he was very, very stubborn. Still, I knew he deserved his happy ending, and I was determined to give it to him.

Eventually the story came together, and this is it. Dante had to rebuild his life, and rediscover joy. Along came Sara, the girl who had gotten away from a teenage Dante many years ago. I hope you enjoy their story.

Best,

Linda

Chapter 1

The doorbell chimed as Sara stepped into a tennis shoe, preparing for her usual evening walk along quiet streets that wound beneath oak trees older than her recently deceased grandfather's grandfather. She muttered an annoyed, "Shoot," and stumbled toward the door with one shoe on and untied and the other clutched in her hand. Opal, invaluable housekeeper, chef and occasional answerer of doorbells, had just left for the day. Didn't that figure?

Sara opened the door, expecting to find a kid selling cookies or band candy, or a neighbor with a complaint or a request, or a Tillman resident with a problem that couldn't wait until morning. From the day she'd agreed to run for office, she'd known being mayor of the small town she'd always called home—in her heart, at least—would be full-time, but she hadn't known exactly *how* full. The fact that more than half the town felt they knew her well enough to drop in unannounced or call at two in the morning didn't help matters any.

What she found on her front porch was none of the ordinary, boring people she'd expected. For a moment, she was speechless.

They just didn't make men like this anymore, did they? Not in Tillman, not anywhere that she'd ever seen. The man on her front porch was the clichéd tall, dark and handsome, wearing a nicely fitted suit and expensive shoes and sporting a head of thick black hair that was conservatively cut but not buzzed to the scalp. One look at his face, and her stomach dropped out from under her. Her toes tingled. Whatever words she should've spoken got stuck in her throat. She should've been better prepared; she'd known she'd see him sooner or later.

Dante Mangino, the object of a long-ago summer romance she'd never been able to forget, shifted his coat jacket aside to reveal the badge attached to his belt. He obviously hadn't recognized her yet, and with a combination of heartbreak and relief she wondered if he'd forgotten all about her. She'd been so worried about running into him down at city hall, she'd played the possibilities of their first encounter in her mind again and again—and he didn't even remember her.

She shouldn't be surprised. After all, they'd been seventeen last time they'd seen one another, a very long eighteen years ago, and while she'd experienced a real, intense love, at least for a while, she'd never fooled herself into thinking that what Dante had felt had been anything more than raging teenage hormones.

He'd changed, just as she had. He was older, bigger,

less pretty and more manly. And he'd cut his hair. Sara tried to convince herself that if she hadn't known Dante was in town, *she* might not recognize *him.*

Since he showed no hint of recollection, she decided to play the game that way. She gathered her composure and smiled politely. "You must be Sergeant Mangino."

"That's me," he answered.

"How nice of you to stop by. I heard you were in town, helping out your cousin Chief Edwards during this unfortunate manpower shortage, and I was hoping we'd get a chance to meet." He'd been in town for two weeks, and until now she'd managed to avoid him. Yes, she'd avoided him at the same time she'd fantasized about their first meeting after all these years. Did that mean she was emotionally twelve years old where he was concerned? How embarrassing. Perhaps it was just as well that they get this over with, once and for all.

Sara opened the door wider and invited him into the foyer, where Vance antiques that had been collected over many years indicated money and influence. Decent money and local influence, at least. She'd inherited everything here, and none of it really felt as if it was hers. She was a keeper. A guardian. "It's nice of you to stop by to introduce yourself. I'm so grateful that you agreed to join us until we can rebuild the department. The chief and I both appreciate your time and sacrifice. This is a difficult time for our city, but we'll soon recover and be all the better for it."

Dante looked confused. His eyes narrowed slightly, his nose wrinkled, and she could see the bewilderment on his face. He had always been so easy to read. For her, at least. His eyes gave away so much. "You're…"

"Mayor Vance." Sara offered her hand, the one that didn't continue to clutch a walking shoe. "It's a pleasure to meet you. I was just on my way out for a walk." She sat in a foyer chair, which was upholstered in a striped fabric, where she slipped on her other shoe and then bent to tie them both. It was good to break eye contact for a moment; good to take the opportunity to take a deep, calming breath. Even after all these years, Dante made her nervous. She could swear that the very air in the house had changed, grown thicker and warmer the moment he'd entered.

As she stared at her shoelaces and pulled one more snugly into place, she said, "If you have any questions about your job here, or if you have any suggestions about the department, please feel free to stop by my office anytime."

It was a dismissal, one anyone in their right mind should recognize, but he didn't move. After a painfully long moment, he said, "I'm not here to introduce myself, Mayor Vance. I'm here about the theft."

Sara took another long, deep breath, but it did nothing to calm her. Great. Not only had some pervert stolen her underwear, she now had to discuss the matter, in detail, with a man who made her nervous. With a drool-worthy guy who'd once had his hand up her blouse and had apparently forgotten. How unflattering. How humiliating. Again she said, "Come by my office in the morning and…"

"Did the crime take place at your office?"

"Of course not," she responded.

"Then why would I want to interview you there?"

Interview. Of course. Dante had come to ask her

about the bras and panties that had been stolen from the clothesline in her backyard. It made sense, she supposed, that he would want to question her here. She should've simply replaced the missing garments and moved on.

"It was no big deal," she said. "Really. I'm sure it was nothing more than a practical joke played by bored kids. There are lots of middle-school-age kids in the neighborhood, and it's just the sort of prank they might think was amusing, stealing the mayor's…underthings."

Dante didn't agree with her and leave her in peace, as he should have. He didn't take another look at her face and ask, "Don't I know you?" The annoying man took a small notepad from his breast pocket and flipped it open. "Three bras and four pairs of panties," he said without blushing or stammering, "valued at four hundred and twenty-five dollars." He flipped the notebook closed with the same grace and ease with which he'd opened it. "That's some fancy underwear, Mayor Vance."

Her face grew hot. She'd been raised in a conservative household, and while she had grown up in an age where almost anything was acceptable and she did not exactly embrace the conservatism of her grandparents, she also didn't feel comfortable discussing her underwear with just anyone. She hadn't seen Dante in eighteen years and he had forgotten her, so he was in fact, not much better than a stranger. "It was good quality, not *fancy*," she responded, proud of herself for not stuttering.

"I'm pretty sure I haven't spent that much on underwear in my entire life."

Sara blinked hard. *Too much information.* "Actually…"

She stood, feeling uncomfortable sitting while Dante—
what was he these days, anyway, six foot three?—towered
over her. "There's no reason to discuss this any further.
I've decided to drop the matter."

"Why?" he asked simply.

"It's not worth the trouble, and I feel terrible that city
time and expense has been wasted on such a trivial matter. I suppose I panicked a bit when I called the police
after my housekeeper discovered the…the…"

"Underwear," he replied when she faltered.

"Was gone," she finished, annoyed to realize that
he could have just as easily supplied the word *theft*.
"This incident is a nuisance, not worth wasting your
valuable time."

That got a very sexy half grin out of Dante. He was
older, bigger, harder, but the grin had not changed. "The
way this city pays its officers, at the present my time's
not all that *valuable*, Mayor Vance," he added belatedly.

Again, he was out of bounds. "While I do appreciate
your help, Sergeant Mangino, the city budget is not something you and I should be discussing," she said primly,
even though getting more money for the city's employees was high on her wish list. The problem was, she
couldn't fabricate the money required out of thin air, and
making budgetary changes was more complicated than
she'd thought it would be. She'd been in office not much
more than two months, and so far it was slow going. Not
that she'd explain any of that to Dante Mangino.

Two things happened at once. Dante turned his head
and she got a glimpse of a tattoo creeping out of his
starched shirt collar. That was new. Tattoos were pretty
much mainstream these days, but they weren't exactly

commonplace among Tillman's city employees. To have one on his neck...

And the doorbell rang. She walked past Dante to answer, staying well out of his way, happy for the chance to walk away from him for a moment so she could regain her composure. Not much rattled her these days, and she needed to get over this silly reaction to a man who was nothing more than an old boyfriend. An old boyfriend who had forgotten her. As Sara reached for the doorknob, she hoped for the band candy or cookies she had expected when Dante had rung the doorbell.

She threw open the door, and at first she saw nothing. No neighbor, no child selling overpriced fundraiser treats she always felt obligated to buy. Then she glanced down and saw the package sitting on the welcome mat. The smallish—no more than eight inches square— package was pretty, wrapped in bright pink paper and accented with a large silver bow and a stripe of matching ribbon. She bent and picked up the box, wondering if a delivery had mistakenly been made to the wrong house. The package was very light, she noted, but was a little heavier than an empty box of this size should be. As she turned she glanced at the small card attached to the bow. No mistake. Her name—Mayor Sarabeth Louann Vance—was written there in a neat script.

"Your birthday?" Dante asked.

"No." Sara pushed the front door closed with a gentle push of her hip, then she placed the box on an antique foyer table, carefully pushing back the flower arrangement there to make room for the unexpected gift.

"Who's it from?" Dante asked sharply.

"I don't know." She carefully opened the dangling card, which bore her name. Inside was blank, and she told him so.

She reached for the bow, but suddenly a large, warm, strong hand clamped over her wrist, stilling her movements. Her heart seemed to catch in her chest, not because someone had left her an anonymous package, but because Dante Mangino had touched her.

"Not a good idea, Mayor," Dante said in a lowered, very dangerous voice that sent a shiver down her spine. He lifted her hand away from the box and dropped it, then fetched a knife from his pocket and opened it with a flick of his thumb.

First he cut the ribbon, then he touched the blade to the end of the box where the paper gapped, barely moving the bright pink wrapping aside with the tip of steel.

"This isn't necessary," she said, her voice purposely tight and mayorlike. She was learning to use that tone when necessary. She used it now to push away the unexpected and unwanted physical reaction that had begun—no, that had spiraled out of control—when Dante had touched her.

"Are you sure?" he asked without turning to look at her. "Are you absolutely positive that this box was left by a well-meaning friend who dropped it on your doorstep, rang the bell and ran?"

"Of course I can't be *sure*," she responded.

"Then unbunch your panties and let me do this my way."

Unbunch her panties? How unprofessional. How ungentlemanly! *Unbunch her panties?* That was the last straw. She should fire him, here and now. He was insolent and unprofessional and having much too much fun at her expense. Plus he had forgotten her, the most egregious sin of all. She tried to imagine looking Dante in the eye and telling him his services were no longer required. Somehow it didn't turn out well, not even in her imagination. Better yet, she could call the chief as soon as Dante left her house and insist that the man be fired by someone else.

The problem was they needed this experienced man on the force until more qualified officers could be hired. Tillman needed Dante Mangino much more than he needed them. He was here because his cousin, the chief, had asked for a favor to help rebuild the department, which had been ravaged by a couple of retirements, three transfers to larger departments in the state and one heart attack.

Dante finally studied the attached card with the tip of his knife. His head rotated slowly and he pinned accusing eyes on her. "Sarabeth Louann Caldwell Vance."

"Yes," she said, trying very hard to remain calm. Caldwell has *not* on the card. At least he remembered her name. "My maiden name was Caldwell." Her mouth went very dry. "Have we met?" The final word came out as a tinny squeak.

He snorted lightly beneath his breath. "You know damn well we have. Sorry, I didn't immediately connect Mayor Sara Vance with the girl of many names, Sarabeth Louann Caldwell. You've changed." He looked her up and down, openly appraising and seemingly approving. "Your hair's lighter and you've put on twenty pounds, all of it in the right places." He grinned, and though he was older, the smile was familiarly

wicked and tempting. "The eyes haven't changed at all.
Neither has the mouth. As soon as you mentioned the
city's 'unfortunate manpower shortage' I knew it was
you. Since you didn't seem to remember me at all, I decided to let it go." He looked her up and down. "You
look good, Sarabeth, and I'm going to kill Jesse for not
telling me exactly who the mayor is these days."

Busted. Dante obviously knew she'd been pretending
not to remember him. At least she could *pretend* not to
be mortified. "Everyone just calls me Sara these days, and
I do hope you won't incapacitate my chief of police over
a simple misunderstanding. I'm sure he doesn't have a
clue that you and I were once friends." After all, they'd
done their best to hide their short relationship from their
friends and families and had done a good job until the
very end. Sara had been the A student, good girl, daughter
of a prominent local family and, yes, rich. Dante had
been in town for the summer to stay with his aunt, uncle
and cousins. He'd driven a motorcycle, worn his hair
long, smoked too much and stayed out too late. They'd
truly had nothing in common, except some perverted
chemistry they never would've discovered if not for a
crazy string of coincidences on one hot summer night.

"Oh, he has more than a clue," Dante said as he returned his attention to the anonymous gift on the table.

Great. All this time and she'd had no idea that her
chief of police knew about her teenage mistake. She'd
made more than one, as most teenagers had, but Dante
was the *big* mistake. Foolish of her to think no one outside a very small circle had known. Even more foolish
of her to think it mattered now, after so many years.

One piece of tape at a time, the package was unwrapped with Dante's little knife. Sara watched as he dissected the paper as if he were a surgeon and the hot-pink wrapping paper, his patient. No move was unsteady or unthinking. The work claimed his entire attention, and she was quite sure he had dismissed her entirely. She might as well have not been in the room at all.

Eventually, he revealed a square, white gift box. He listened to the box, hefted it with the tip of his knife, turned it this way and that, and eventually opened it with the same calculating blade he had used to remove the pink paper.

Fine, dark eyebrows lifted. "Oh," he muttered as he looked down into the box.

Sara moved to stand beside him, since there was obviously no danger. She reached forward, but again Dante stopped her with that strong hand of his. "No touching," he said. "There might be prints."

Sara sighed. "Yes, I'm sure the state lab will be anxious to get right on that. Alert, alert," she said, rolling her eyes. "Drop those murder cases and get right on this anonymous gift of…" she glanced into the box to spy a jumbled mixture of fine, brightly colored silk. Dante reached into the box with his knife and pulled out a demicup red silk bra adorned with a smattering of black lace. The bra dangled from the short, sharp blade.

"Your size?" he asked.

She glanced at the tag and felt her insides drop. "Yes. But seriously, we don't have our own fingerprinting facilities, and by the time the state lab gets around to something like this, whatever crime has been committed will be well beyond the statute of limitations."

"I'm not sending it to the state lab," he said as he returned the bra to the box. "I work for a top-notch private firm, when I'm not doing one family member or another a favor. The Benning Agency has a more than competent facility and crew. They can handle a little fingerprinting." He looked down at her. "The undergarments will all be ruined in the process." His knife blade entered the box again, and he came out with an absurdly insubstantial pair of panties that matched the demibra. "So if you'd rather keep these…"

"No!" she responded hotly, stepping away from Dante and the box. "I'm not going to wear underwear that's been left on my doorstep by a pervert who obviously has some kind of fetish."

He returned the panties to the box and came up again with an emerald-green bra no more ample than the red one. "A fetish and very good taste."

Dante dropped the green bra into the box. So far this was the most interesting crime he'd investigated since coming to the small town of Tillman, Alabama. Just last week he'd nabbed a thief who'd tried to make his getaway on a riding lawn mower. Even when the moron had realized he was being followed, he hadn't stopped, not even to dump his pillowcase full of loot. There had been a nasty fight at the barbershop over a really bad haircut, and a tussle over a prime parking spot in front of the drug store.

And now this. For his newest assignment he'd be hunting down a creep or creeps who stole underwear and replaced it with sexier stuff. Not that he'd seen what had been stolen from her clothesline, but judging by what little he remembered of Sarabeth Caldwell—

now Sara Vance—he suspected her drawers—of the furniture sort—were filled with sensible and sturdy underwear that held everything firmly in place. Personally, he liked a little jiggle. Lovely extra pounds aside, Sara looked as if she avoided jiggling at all cost.

It had been a real shock when she'd looked at him just so and pursed her lips and the past had come rushing back. In his mind Sarabeth—Sara—had remained seventeen, skinny and young and timid. To see her in this woman, to instantly have that part of his life come rushing back, had given him a jolt. Fortunately he was much better at hiding his emotions than he'd been at seventeen.

Jesse deserved an ass-whoopin' for this one. When he'd handed over the slim file on this case, he could've warned his unsuspecting cousin that the mayor was the young, beautiful woman Dante had once made out with in a '72 Camaro that had not afforded him nearly enough maneuvering room, as he remembered. He had heard that the mayor was a widow, and with a common name like Sara he had suspected she'd be an older woman, one who'd taken up local politics in retirement. No wonder the other investigators didn't want this job. How could any red-blooded man look at Sara Vance and talk about her bras and panties and not get, well, a bit flustered?

Dante didn't fluster easily, not even when he had to face down a pretty woman who stammered when she said *underwear,* who looked naturally sexy with her dark blond hair in a thick ponytail and her T-shirt stretched over nicely shaped breasts encased in what appeared to be, from his vantage point, a very sturdy bra, who had changeable and smart blue eyes that revealed everything. Surprise, annoyance, anger…even a woman's reluctant interest in a man. He'd seen her interest, as well as her disapproval as her eyes had fallen on the curling end of the tattoo that crawled across his shoulder and partway up his neck.

Pretty or not, Sarabeth Louann Caldwell Vance—how many names did any one woman need, anyway?—was not the kind of woman he'd tangle with. This house and her demeanor screamed old money, her position in politics screamed old power. The set of her mouth and the glint in her eyes screamed, "Interested or not, I don't fall easily, not anymore. If you think you're going to feel me up again, you are sadly mistaken." No, she wouldn't fall, not into bed, not into relationships, short or long. Dante was definitely into easy, at least where women were concerned.

The thought sounded shallow and callous, even to him, but it was honest enough. He hadn't fought for anything or anyone that wasn't assigned by the Benning Agency for a very long time.

"I'm going for my walk, now," Sara said, her voice almost prim as she dismissed him and the box. "If I don't hurry, I won't get home before dark."

"Wait one minute while I get a pair of gloves from the car."

She sighed as if waiting for such a short period of time would be an imposition, and then curtly nodded her head in agreement.

When Dante returned, white gloves on so he could handle the box and wrapping paper without leaving his own prints, he could tell that Sara had gathered herself more staunchly together. Whatever interest might've once been visible in her eyes was gone, and her chin and mouth seemed to be set more staunchly—more mayor-like. Even her spine was a bit straighter, a bit harder. She had her house keys in one hand and wore an expression that said, *Thank you for your service, now get out.*

Was she always so unyielding, or was this attitude just for him? They'd shared a few weeks of teenage passion years ago, but he was not the same person he'd been at seventeen. Neither was she.

They exited the front door together, she, locking the door behind her, he, gingerly handling the evidence. She was right: the state lab would laugh at his request if he asked them to print all of this for a panty thief. Bennings, however, had a fairly new and not badly equipped lab, along with a couple of geeks to play with all the toys.

Still, explaining this one wasn't going to be easy.

He carefully stored the evidence in the trunk of his city-issued unmarked car, a boring, dependable, burgundy Crown Vic. Sara remained close by, tapping her toes, as if anxious for him to leave. Now that they were out of the house, she didn't have to remain with him until he left, but she seemed compelled to do so. Some "good manners" thing, he supposed.

Dante slammed the trunk and then caught her eye. Crap. She was probably right about this, too. The man he was looking for was likely a perv who was into the new mayor and didn't know any other way to express his affection, such as it was. The crime, his first real investigative case in Tillman, was creepy but probably perfectly harmless.

Probably. He often worked as a bodyguard for the

Benning Agency, so he'd dealt with more than one
stalker, more than one perv whose actions went above
and beyond what any sane person would think of. It was
a mistake to believe that those on the other side of the
law would always think and behave rationally. They
didn't, and the results could be—had been—deadly. It
had been a long time since he'd seen the world through
naive eyes.

"You walk every day?" he asked.

"Yes," she said in a polite but emotionally distant voice.

"Same time every day?"

"Close enough," she said, her brow wrinkling.

Dante looked her up and down. "I don't suppose I
could talk you into skipping your walk today." It would
soon enough be dark, and while the neighborhood appeared to be peaceful, someone had just dumped a box
full of sexy underwear on her doorstep and then run
from the scene.

"No," she answered sharply. "This is all very strange,
but I won't be scared into hiding in my house. Besides,
I need the exercise."

"I'll buy you a treadmill."

She laughed, and then apparently decided she'd
stuck around long enough in the name of courtesy. Sara
turned away and headed down the sidewalk, her step
brisk, her head back, her hips set into intriguing motion.

"Still want to drop this case?" he called after her, his
eyes focused on the sway of her hips.

"I suppose not," she answered reluctantly, not slow-
ing down, not looking back.

Dante sighed and got behind the wheel of the Crown
Vic. He'd rather be in his own pickup truck, but Jesse

had insisted. The job came with rules that required a haircut, a suit, a tie and this old woman's car. Jesse was doing a lot of insisting these days for someone who had asked for such a huge favor.

The mayor didn't look back, not even when Dante cranked the engine. He watched her for a moment, mentally marking Sara as trouble of the worst sort, mentally cursing Jesse for throwing him into this case without warning, mentally undressing the staid politician and wondering what she'd look like in that green silk bra and matching panties. Yes, she'd been a skinny teenage girl when last he'd touched her, but she'd filled out in all the right places.

Dante cursed succinctly, and then he rolled down the street, following the woman who steadfastly refused to look back.

Chapter 2

So, maybe she should've taken Dante's advice and stayed in tonight. Usually, Sara relaxed completely when she walked. Usually, she didn't think about anything but the beauty of the old trees and houses that lined the streets in this part of town, the fresh air that filled her lungs—and maybe that pair of black dress pants she wanted to get back into, and wouldn't if she didn't get enough exercise. Five pounds would do it. Maybe ten. Dante might think differently, but as far as she was concerned there was no such thing as the right place on her body for twenty pounds.

Of course, he wasn't as thin as he'd once been, either, but it looked as if everything he'd added was muscle. Every change made him look more handsome, more manly. His jaw seemed sharper, his nose slightly more prominent and yet as straight and perfect as ever. There was muscle in his neck and a power to his hands that made it clear he was no longer a child. There was less softness in his face and his body, less vulnerability in his eyes. She knew no specifics, but she got the sense that life had not been entirely kind to Dante.

Just minutes after leaving her house, she wished with all she had that she'd stayed at home. In the last light of day she noticed every shadow and wondered if someone was hiding within one. She heard every chirping bird, every barking dog, every creak, and she imagined the worst. She walked a little bit faster, but that did nothing to change the shadows and the alarming noises. The hairs on the back of her neck seemed to rise up, and her heartbeat increased for reasons other than exercise.

A treadmill, Dante had suggested. Maybe that wasn't such a bad idea.

Lydia and Patty had accused her, on more than one occasion, of being perverse. If someone said she shouldn't do something, she had to give it a try. Robert hadn't called her perverse, but he had more than once accused her of being stubborn as all get out. Her husband had been gone for four years, gone much too soon, and there were still times that she thought of him and it hurt like hell. She'd decided that the pain—a pain that came less often when she kept herself too busy to think about Robert and all they'd missed—would never go away.

Perverse or stubborn as all get out, those who knew her best said. So, was she walking down a deserted street at dusk simply because a man who made her anxious and twitchy had suggested that she not?

Suddenly, she was positive someone was following

her. It wasn't her imagination, not anymore. She heard a car engine, but no car went past her. The engine was almost idling, the car moved so slowly. The motor purred and whispered, instead of racing as a car engine should. Her neck and the palms of her hands itched. Her heart pounded and her mouth went dry. She listened for the car to stop at the curb. She listened for the driver to get out and walk to the door of one of the houses she walked past so she could dismiss her worry as silly and unnecessary.

No. Someone had anonymously sent her sexy underwear, in the right size no less, so her worries were not silly. Not silly at all. Had her underwear thief stolen the things that had been drying on the line simply to get her size? That indicated an unhealthy interest and determination and all the other traits one did not want from a secret admirer. Like it or not, she could not brush this incident off as nothing. Not anymore. She took a deep breath, gathered her composure as best she could and turned her head slowly, trying for a nonchalant glance back. She'd pretend to see a neighbor. Maybe she'd even look past the car to smile and wave. Surely if someone was following her they wouldn't try anything if they knew they'd been seen.

Sara took a deep breath, slowed her step and turned her head—and was immediately relieved *and* incensed. How dare he? She spun about and stalked toward the car that was so obviously tailing her as if she were the criminal.

Dante Mangino smiled and lifted the fingers that had been resting on the steering wheel of his city car for a casual wave. He didn't even have the grace to look guilty! Conservative suit and short haircut aside, he didn't look like any police officer she'd ever seen. He was irreverent, fiery—and, after all these years, still the bad boy.

The driver's-side window was down, allowing him to enjoy the mild March air. One arm rested nonchalantly there, his elbow jutting out of the car.

"What do you think you're doing?" she asked.

He didn't seem at all taken aback by her obvious annoyance. "Why, ma'am, I'm making sure the mayor of this fine town gets home safe and sound. That's all."

Was it her imagination, or was his subtle Southern accent exaggerated a bit for that comment?

Sara's first impulse was to tell him that it was unnecessary, and then she admitted to herself that she was comforted to see him there, that the shadows did not seem so ominous now that she was not alone, and the noises that had moments earlier seemed out of place were suddenly ordinary and not at all alarming.

"This is ridiculous," she said in a calm voice. "The least you can do is park your car, get out and walk with me." She could only imagine what her neighbors would have to say about that, but it was preferable to having him tail her around the block at three miles an hour.

It was obvious by Dante's expression that he had not expected the invitation. He'd expected—perhaps even wanted—a fight.

"All right," he said, pulling his car closer to the curb and shutting off the engine. He exited the car in a way that was smooth and graceful and strong. She wasn't sure how that was possible, but it was. This man, Chief Jesse Edwards's cousin or not, was trouble with a capital *T*.

After the disaster with Dante so many years ago,

Sara had worked very hard to be immune to trouble, especially of the male kind. While her friends in college had gone gaga over bad boys with pretty faces, she had always looked for more. She'd looked for intelligence and a sense of humor and kindness. She'd looked for stability. After her brief and fabulous and ultimately unhappy experience with Dante, those were the attributes she deemed to be worthy, not killer dark eyes and a face with sharp lines and nicely shaped lips, and thick heads of hair that might be a warm black or a very dark brown. Not long legs and strong hands and a way of moving that was both graceful and masculine. Those things were nice bonuses, but they were shallow and not at all important.

So why did her mouth go dry as Dante Mangino approached? "You're not really dressed for walking."

"That's not a problem," he said, and then he smiled. "You don't walk very fast."

Sara resumed her walk. With Dante beside her she felt much less anxious in one way—and much more uneasy in another. She couldn't allow a man to get under her skin so easily. Her memories of the past were just that—memories of a time gone by. She was not the same person she'd been at seventeen, and neither was he. She didn't know him at all. Dante was still good-looking, and he was in great physical shape—and he had no manners at all. He had a wicked grin and a way of taking her breath away with a glance.

For so long—from the time she'd met Robert eleven years ago, in fact—her relationships with men other than her husband had been businesslike or comfortably casual. She'd never met any man who made her feel so on edge, so anxious. Sara was old enough and experienced enough to know what that edgy feeling meant.

In an instant, Dante Mangino had reawakened a part of her that had been sleeping for such a long time she'd thought it dead and gone.

It would be best to quickly and firmly put him in that business category, to squash whatever it was he aroused in her. "So," she said casually as they walked down the familiar sidewalk. "Tell me about yourself. Are you married?" She hoped he'd say yes. No matter how attractive he was, no matter how he turned her stomach to mush with a glance, no matter that she still remembered what his arms felt like when they wrapped around her, she would not even consider getting involved with or even fantasizing about a married man.

"Nope," he answered. He matched her short strides with his long ones with little effort, and offered no details or other information about himself.

"I imagine you have a serious girlfriend," she said. As long as he was in some sort of committed relationship…

"No," he said, as decisively as he'd denied being married.

She *knew* he wasn't gay. Too bad. That would definitely solve her problem. She was a sensible woman. Why had she felt drawn to this man from the moment she'd opened the door? She didn't believe in instant attraction! It was too much like love at first sight, which she most definitely did not believe in. She and Robert had been friends first, good friends, and love had come later. It had grown slowly and surely into something special.

Robert had been a lasting, slow burn. Dante had been a firecracker.

"Why the interest in my personal life, Mayor?" Dante asked.

Did he address her as "Mayor" in order to maintain a distance? Was he as uninterested in rekindling what they'd had as she was? It wasn't as if they'd seen one another and fallen into welcoming arms. "I'm just trying to be friendly, to catch up. After all, we haven't seen each other in a long time. I'm simply making conversation, and you're not helping with your one-word answers."

"Sorry," he responded, not sounding at all remorseful. "So, let's catch up. Are you dating anyone? Is there a guy around who would love to see you in that teeny-weeny red silk…"

"Dante Mangino!" Sara snapped. "That is…" she stammered and her step faltered. "That question is so inappropriate, I don't know how to respond."

"Yes or no will do," he said, his step and his voice maddeningly steady. "After all, we're just making conversation. Just catching up." There was an edge to his voice as he threw her words back at her.

"Perhaps we shouldn't bother," she muttered. As they rounded the corner she was glad for the ensuing silence. She and Dante had nothing in common these days. They never had! Yes, he was good-looking and a fine example of the male species, but if she had to spend more than a few minutes alone with him, he'd quickly drive her crazy. Of course, they wouldn't necessarily have to talk… Sara started counting her steps to lead her mind in another direction.

"Is there a boyfriend?" her walking companion asked a short while later, his voice deeper and more thoughtful than it had been before.

"I don't see that it's an issue."

"A boyfriend or ex should be the first suspect in a theft like yours. The angle is very personal, very intimate."

At least he didn't say *underwear* again. "No boyfriend," she said. "No ex, either," she added before he could ask.

"That surprises me," he said, sounding momentarily sincere.

"I'm a widow."

"I know. Sorry." His words were simple and short but seemed heartfelt. "So, no boyfriends at all since your husband died?"

"Robert's been gone four years." Four years, three months and seven days, to be precise. "No, there hasn't been anyone since then." That sting in her heart flared up again. The ache always caught her by surprise, though by now she should be used to it.

"How about unwanted attention?" Dante asked. "Has anyone been asking you out repeatedly, hanging around, sending gifts, writing letters?"

Since he sounded as if he was thinking strictly of business, she did not take offense. "No." Then she laughed lightly and added, "Unless you count anonymous letters telling me what a terrible mayor I am and how a woman has no business in the office and how…"

Dante stopped in his tracks. "Anonymous letters?"

Sara stopped, too. They had almost completed her usual circuitous course, and she could see her house two doors down. It was all but dark, and where the oaks shadowed her house and the street it truly was night. "It comes with the job."

"Do any of these letters threaten violence?" Dante snapped.

"No. They're simply the ramblings of dissatisfied residents of Tillman who're too cowardly to sign their names."

Her escort took her arm and led her toward her house. "Did you keep the letters?"

"Yes. I file all correspondence." He was moving a little bit too fast for her. With his quick step and long legs and the way he held her arm, she had to almost jog to keep pace.

"Tomorrow morning I'd like a look at those letters."

"Why? They can't possibly be related to the theft."

"Can't possibly?" he repeated. "Are you sure?"

She didn't have an answer for that, so she remained silent as he steered her with purpose toward her own front door.

After driving around the block a couple of times and then grabbing a coffee and sandwich to go at the Tillman Café, Dante parked at the curb in front of the mayor's house. He was probably being overly cautious, but in his world that was much preferable to not being cautious enough. He'd had the world yanked out from under him once before and wouldn't allow that to happen again. It was easiest to expect and be prepared for the worst.

When he got a look at the letters in the morning, he'd have a better idea about whether or not he should be concerned. Working for Bennings, he was usually called in after the case had turned serious. He wasn't sure how to handle something that might be threatening but was more likely to be nothing at all.

By nine-thirty, all the downstairs lights in Sara Vance's house were out. There were outdoor lights that remained on for security purposes, but he could easily see the interior illumination through the windows, and one by one the lamps and overhead lights were extinguished. He could imagine Sara climbing the stairs, drawing a bath—or did she prefer a shower?—then climbing into bed with a book or maybe some work she'd brought home with her. What would she sleep in? he wondered. Flannel pajamas, maybe. A long, prim nightgown with a drawstring in the hem. Then again, perhaps she had a secret wild side and slept in red satin or, even better, nothing at all. The prim presentation could be a front, a facade that kept unwanted attention at a distance.

You must be Sergeant Mangino, my ass.

Her bedroom faced the street. At least, Dante assumed it was her bedroom, since that was where the last light of the night remained on. Yeah, that was her bedroom. He could see no more than lacy, feminine curtains, and still, he knew. She was there, sitting up in her bed with that book or papers from work in her lap. Maybe there was a television in that room and she was catching the news.

Sitting alone in his car, he smiled. Maybe he hadn't recognized her right away, but he would never forget Sarabeth Caldwell and those few weeks they'd spent so much time together. They had run in such dissimilar circles that they never should've met, but in a small town it had been inevitable.

Her date at a summer party for the popular kids—a

party Dante had crashed, thanks to cousin Jesse—had drunk too much beer and had ended up making out with one of Sarabeth's friends. Moron. The other girl had been easy and, as he remembered, well developed, but she had not been nearly as pretty as Sarabeth.

He remembered stepping outside to smoke and finding her, shoulders shaking and face in hands. For a moment he'd considered sneaking back into the house before she saw him, but instead he'd offered to drive her home.

She'd quickly said yes because she hadn't wanted to go back into the party and let the others see her cry. The fact that *he* had seen her crying hadn't seemed to matter. He had been temporary. In a few weeks he'd be gone, and it wasn't as though there had been anyone of importance that he could have told about her embarrassment. He'd known that and hadn't cared. There was no way he could've left her there, alone and miserable, hiding and suffering.

He'd taken Jesse's keys and promised to be back in a matter of minutes. The flat tire could not have come at a better time.

Dante had changed the tire, and Sarabeth had quit crying. She'd gotten angry and accused him of causing the flat tire. He'd laughed at her and she hadn't liked that at all. These days he could easily arrange a convenient flat tire, with some planning and the right tools, but back then he hadn't had a clue. He hadn't had a clue about a lot of things, truth be told.

Somewhere along the way, he'd kissed Sarabeth. It hadn't been his first kiss, or hers, but he could still remember kissing her and feeling as if he was falling into nothingness, like nothing else mattered. She'd been a spoiled rich kid who would never have looked his way if she hadn't needed him, and he'd suspected that the kiss was a revenge of sorts for the cheating boyfriend. None of that had mattered, however, and that kiss had changed everything.

Only one other time in his life had he found himself attracted to a woman who was so totally and completely wrong for him. Whatever contentment he'd found in thinking of the old days with Sarabeth disappeared in a flash as he stared at the house before him and let go of old memories.

Things hadn't worked out well for Serena. Not at all. Dante didn't waste his time on women like her—or Sara—anymore. He wasn't so foolish as to think that he could bring a woman into the world he lived in and then let her go unscathed. Or worse, never let her go at all.

The women who came into and out of his life on a regular basis knew who he was and what he wanted and that he wouldn't be sticking around for long, and they didn't care. They lived for the moment, for the night. Four years after her husband's passing, Sara Vance remained faithful. She likely could not even imagine living for the night, giving herself to a man who wouldn't stay, throwing herself into the moment strictly for the fun of it. For the pleasure.

Even eighteen years ago she'd been cautious. They'd kissed plenty, and he'd snaked his hand up her blouse more than once, but that had been it. He'd thought he'd die if he didn't have her, if he didn't get inside her, but she would have none of it. They'd come close, very close, but in the end Sarabeth Caldwell had been the one to get away, the one female he'd wanted to distraction and had not had. Maybe that was lucky for her.

Around ten-fifteen, the light in her bedroom was switched off. A moment later, the lace curtains at that window moved, very slightly. Was she watching him, now? Did she realize or care that he was keeping an eye on her?

The curtain fell, and he waited. Knowing Sara, she was likely to come storming out of the house in a thick, ugly bathrobe, still managing to look sexy as all get out. She'd order him off her street. She'd order him to go back to his lonely little duplex and get some sleep. When that didn't happen, he waited for his cell to ring. She was the mayor, after all, and getting his cell number from Jesse wouldn't take her more than a few minutes.

But no one came running out of the house, and his phone didn't ring. Maybe she hadn't seen him after all.

It was after midnight when Dante finally headed toward his rented duplex to grab a few hours of sleep. He was restless, unsettled. It had been a while since he'd thought about Serena. As he drove down the deserted Tillman streets, he wondered if he'd dream of colorful silk and creamy skin, or slit throats and unheard screams.

When the door to her office opened without warning, Sara's head snapped up. After yesterday evening's disturbing events, she was more than a little on edge. Jumpy. She was downright jumpy. She was relieved to see her friend Patty walk in, bearing two tall disposable cups of coffee. Dressed for work in a conservative blue suit, with her long dark hair pulled back into a sleek bun, Patty looked very much the professional. There was no hint of the wild child she had once been—not outwardly.

A couple times a week, Patty stopped by on her way to work at the bank. They had coffee and talked for a few minutes. Now that Patty was married, they didn't get to spend as much time together as they had when Patty had been single and sworn off men, and Sara had been widowed less than a year and newly relocated to Tillman. Sara would never begrudge her friend happiness, but she did miss those days when they'd spent so much time together. Much of that time had been spent convincing themselves that they did not need or want male companionship of any sort. She'd actually believed that for a long time.

"The highlights look good," Patty said.

Sara patted her tightly restrained hair. "I had it done Friday afternoon. You don't think it's too much?" For years she'd worried more than she should about her image. As a Caldwell, as a Vance, as the wife of an assistant district attorney—as mayor. She wore conservative suits that never felt quite right and fashionable shoes that too often pinched her toes. It came with the job, she told herself.

"Not at all. It's cute." Patty looked Sara up and down in that way only a good friend could, and her smile faded. "You didn't sleep well last night."

Sara sighed. "No, I didn't."

"I warned you being mayor wouldn't be a bed of roses."

"Many times," Sara said with a smile as she took a sip of her coffee. She sighed in delight. The coffee from Bubba's Quick Stop was so much better than the sludge her secretary made every morning. Patty sat in the chair on the opposite side of the desk, and Sara relaxed. This would likely be the most pleasant part of her day, so she might as well enjoy it. "It wasn't exactly city business that kept me up half the night," she confessed.

Something in her voice grabbed Patty's attention. The woman's eyes sparkled. Aah, yes, there was that hint of the wild child. Her spine straightened. Her lips curved into a smile. "What's going on?"

Being very careful with her words, Sara told her friend about everything that had happened yesterday. She tried not to make Dante sound too interesting, or even to make him a too-important part of the story. He was ancillary, a necessary evil, no different than any other officer who might've been investigating her case. Patty had moved to Tillman her senior year of high school, months after the fiasco with Dante had ended, and there had been no reason to tell her—or anyone else—what had happened. So Sara told the story as if she'd never seen Dante before yesterday.

She did, however, have to end the telling with her looking out of her bedroom window late at night and seeing his car sitting on the street, and she also had to admit that she'd felt comforted at the sight.

"And you didn't call me?" Patty asked, incensed.

"It was too late."

"You could've called me long before you saw the car on the street. Someone delivers replacement undies, very nice stuff to hear you tell it, to your house and you don't even *call?*"

"You have supper at your in-laws every Tuesday," Sara argued.

"And I'm always happy to be interrupted," Patty replied. Her eyes narrowed. "There's more. There's something you're not telling me. This Dante Mangino." She leaned back in her chair and took a sip of coffee. "Tell me about him."

"There's really nothing to tell," Sara said. "He's Chief Edwards's cousin. Apparently he has a lot of experience and has agreed to stay on for a while and help with training and investigations."

"So why is he sitting outside your window late at night? Was it creepy?" Her eyes widened. "Oh, do you think he's the underwear thief?"

"No!"

"If this was a movie, he'd be the one," Patty argued. "He's new in town, there's the underwear theft, sexy stuff is delivered while he's there, you see him watching your house late at night…"

"If it's Dante, then who left the box and rang the doorbell while he was standing in my foyer?"

Patty grimaced. "A small detail easily explained away. Somehow."

"Dante is just…he worries too much, I suppose." Sara gave a nonchalant wave of her hand, doing her best to dismiss the man in every way. "He sees a shadow and he believes there's a danger in it. He sees the worst possible scenario in everything he runs across. A couple of unhappy letters and a panty thief, and he's got me under surveillance." If not for him, she wouldn't even be worried about the letters or the underwear. A little bothered, maybe, but not really *worried.*

Patty cocked her head. "You're already calling this Mangino character by his first name. That's rather interesting, knowing you and the way your brain works. Hmm. You also very quickly and decisively dismissed him as a suspect. What does he look like? Is he as hot as his cousin?"

Hotter. "I suppose some women would think he's attractive, in a...different sort of way from Jesse Edwards."

"Different how?" Patty could be very persistent.

"Just different."

Patty smiled. "You like him, don't you?"

"I do not."

"You do. You've got that little twitch to your lips. It's a dead giveaway. I haven't seen that twitch since college!" Patty's grin was insanely wide. "When do I get to meet him?"

Never, if I have anything to say about it. "I'm sure you'll run into him eventually," Sara said, cursing the ease with which her old friend could read her. A twitch? Why hadn't anyone ever told her she had a twitch? "He's going to be around until I can come up with more money for payroll and Chief Edwards hires more qualified men."

Patty ignored the subject change to city business. "How serious is it? Are we talking love at first sight?"

Sara sighed and drank more coffee. It was a nice little stall but didn't last long enough. Finally she said, "There's nothing at all *serious* going on here, and even if there were, I don't believe in love at first sight and you know it."

"Lust at first sight?" Patty asked without pause.

Again, Sara hesitated. She didn't believe in that, either, not for a woman thirty-five years old. Not for a woman who'd had her heart broken, first by desertion by choice and later by desertion by death. "I don't know," she said softly. "Maybe I was just having an off day." Maybe, even though she did her best to dismiss it as unimportant, the theft and anonymous gift had rattled her more than she'd realized, and a capable man, any capable man, was a comfort.

Maybe she'd simply been alone too long.

Natalie Douglas, Sara's secretary and maker of terrible coffee, knocked briefly and then opened the door. The young woman was truly beautiful, with pale blond hair stylishly cut, cool gray eyes and a figure any woman would kill for. She was also a more than capable assistant and a whiz with computers. If they could just get past the bad coffee thing...

"There's a Sergeant Mangino here to see you. Should I tell him to wait?"

"No!" Patty said with a smile. "Bring him to us immediately."

Natalie ignored Patty's enthusiastic direction and looked to her boss for an answer, and after a moment Sara nodded her head. "Send him in."

Patty's smile widened, and Natalie cast a furtive and blatantly interested glance over her shoulder. Did Dante have this effect on every woman he met? Probably. She should consider that fair warning where he was concerned.

Natalie opened the office door wider, and Dante stepped inside. He glared down at the cup of coffee he had foolishly poured himself in the outer office. "Good God, you could tar a roof with this."

Whenever Sara had carefully and kindly mentioned that perhaps Natalie could make the coffee less strong, the woman had been insulted. Now she took the cup from Dante's hand and promised, in a heartfelt, apologetic voice, to pour it all out and make a better pot. When he added a "Thanks, darlin'," Natalie actually blushed and bit her lower lip in a coy manner.

Sara was momentarily ashamed of her own gender.

Dante nodded to Patty, who all but dropped her jaw at the sight of him. Yes, he was studly, but really…get a grip.

"Do you have those letters?" he asked without preamble, his attention entirely focused on Sara.

"I gathered them together first thing." She handed over the thin stack, certain he wouldn't find anything alarming but not altogether sorry that he was going to check to be sure. Dante shook his head at her as he put on a pair of gloves. Only then did he take the stack of letters.

Patty stood. "I have to go or I'll be late for work. Don't forget the sock burning. Saturday night, Lydia's place, just after dark."

"I'll be there," Sara said.

Patty closed the door on her way out, and when she was gone Dante lifted his head to look at Sara. "Sock burning?"

She gave him a genuine smile. "It's a tradition a couple of friends and I have. Every spring, we gather up all the mismatched socks we've managed to accumulate during the year, and we burn them. Lydia lives outside town on a large piece of property. We build a bonfire and ceremoniously dispose of the socks whose mates went missing in the dryer or just got lost or damaged along the way. Except that year we were having such a drought. We skipped the sock burning that year."

"I have a similar tradition," Dante deadpanned. "I throw mismatched socks in the trash."

Must be a man thing. Robert had voiced the same thought, a time or two, back in the days when the bonfires had been planned around infrequent trips home to see family and friends. He had never understood or embraced the annual sock burning, but he had tolerated the event with a smile. Sara remembered well. She thought of Robert and she smiled herself, and this time his memory didn't hurt. "Where's the fun in that?"

"I didn't know there had to be fun involved in disposing of…" He stopped abruptly and began carefully riffling through the letters. "Never mind. I should know by now never to question a woman's logic since there usually is none."

She could argue that point with him, but chose not to. Not now, at least. "What do you do for fun these days?" The question was out of her mouth before she had time to think it through.

He didn't hesitate to answer. "My idea of fun includes explosives and big guns, or copious amounts of alcohol and loose women." He glanced up, pinning those dark eyes on her. "And in case you're wondering, no. The two various forms of recreation don't mix."

"Good to know," she said softly. Her voice took on a different tone as she asked, "Will there be anything else? I have a busy morning planned."

Dante very gently shook the letters in her direction. "No, this'll do it. Have a good day." He dismissed her and turned just as Natalie opened the door. The smitten secretary held a foam cup of steaming coffee in one hand.

"I hope you like this better," she said sweetly. Too sweetly.

Dante smiled at her. "I'm sure I will, darlin'."

It took all Sara's willpower not to snort out loud.

And once the door closed, her first thought was that Dante Mangino had never called her *darlin'*.

Chapter 3

There was nothing even remotely alarming in the letters Sara had saved. They were all about potholes and city parks, annual festivals and liquor sales. The letters contained no threats, unless you counted the ominous "I will never vote for you again."

The sexy undies that had been dropped on Sara's porch were on their way to Bennings' lab for fingerprinting. Some moron with a sick sense of humor was likely having a bit of fun with the mayor, but when Dante showed up on his doorstep, the fun would end.

The mayor's office was up one flight of stairs and down one long hallway. Dante was tempted to return the letters to Sara personally, just to see for himself that she was all right. Dumb idea. She was fine. A twisted admirer had stolen her underwear and then replaced it, either because he felt guilty about the theft or because he wanted to envision her in the colorful silk. Either way, there was no danger here, no need for his concern.

Maybe he was overly cautious, but he had one woman's death on his head and he wouldn't let that happen again. His internal alarm system was usually accurate, but it had been known to malfunction on occasion. That internal alarm was malfunctioning now, screaming at him because he found himself comparing Sara and Serena in too many ways.

The afternoon was spent training a couple of the newer guys, two cousins not entirely unlike Dante and Jesse, as they had been many years ago. Billy Nance and Sammy Bender were young and eager and more than a little bit competitive. Billy was blond and blue-eyed; Sammy was darker and more intense. They would make good cops if they decided to stick with it.

Training, Dante could handle. He actually relished the work because it allowed him to focus his attentions on someone and something other than the mayor and her panty thief. Since he'd been with Bennings from the beginning, he had often been involved in training. The recruits for the Benning Agency were usually older and more experienced than these guys, but they were no less dedicated. Of course, most of the Benning agents were there for the money, while Billy and Sammy were relentlessly dedicated and hopelessly green, ready and willing to save the world.

Dante enjoyed showing the cousins—the hard way—how ill-prepared they were for physical attack. He liked surprising them with new and unexpected moves, and he really liked it when he saw the ah-ha moment on their faces and knew they'd gotten what he was trying to teach them. If their careers kept them in Tillman, it was possible they would never be in a situation that required these skills. Still, a man could never be too prepared, even if he lived and worked in a town where the last exchanged gunfire left no one so much as scratched, and afterward both men involved had rushed to the police station to file a complaint against the other party. It wasn't a bad way to live, if you could stand the lack of excitement. Dante wasn't sure he could. Working for Bennings for so long had turned him into a danger junkie. He needed the rush of adrenaline, the accelerated heartbeat, the uncertainty.

Even though throughout the afternoon the green recruits both ended up in the air and on their backs—multiple times—they remained eager to learn and willing to take whatever punishment was necessary to prepare themselves for what might come their way. When Billy managed to toss his instructor to his back, through the rush of pain Dante felt like a proud papa.

The chief met Dante as training finished for the day. His cousin wore a wide smile. Jesse had always been the golden boy of the family, and that had not changed. He'd married a sweet girl who'd dutifully given birth to two sons and a daughter. He'd been a detective in Birmingham for years before taking the job here in Tillman, coming home like a good son and making his mama proud.

When Billy and Sammy were on their way back to the station, breathless and exhilarated and out of hearing range, Jesse said, "Aunt Debra loves the haircut. She says it makes you look years younger, and maybe now you can get a woman."

Dante glared. "Where is she?"

"No need to look over your shoulder," Jesse said with a grin. "Your mom's still in Florida. We sent her a picture."

Dante could not remember having his picture taken since getting the haircut required for this job. He could only imagine his mother's delight. They didn't speak often, but when they did, his hair, a job she could explain to her friends, the right kind of woman and the grandchildren she did not have were always subjects of conversation. "How?"

"Janice took a shot with her cell phone when you were over for supper last week. She sent it to Aunt Debra by e-mail."

"I hate technology," Dante said as he headed for his car.

Jesse laughed and followed. He was likely waiting for Dante to say something, anything, about the mayor. Jesse was the only person in the world who knew about what happened that summer. He was also the only person in the world who knew how Dante had felt about Sarabeth Caldwell, way back when. Dante didn't alleviate his cousin's curiosity about the reunion. Jesse had obviously thought it would be a great joke to send Dante in unprepared. He could stew a while.

"Want to come by for supper tonight?" Jesse asked. "Ethan has baseball practice, but he'll be finished by six."

"No, thanks," Dante said.

"You're just mad because Janice told you that you can't use the *s* word or the *f* word at a Little League game."

"Or any of the *c* words," Dante added. "Besides, I only slipped up once, and none of the kids heard me."

"No, but one of the mothers did," Jesse said with a grin. "She went straight to Janice, too."

Which is likely why Janice had snapped a photo and sent it to his mother. Revenge. "I have plans."

"What kind of plans?"

"A run. A shower. A quick supper. Simple." Maybe not so simple if he worked in an evening stroll with the mayor. He'd probably ride by her place. He'd probably stop if he saw her leave the house. He'd probably drive around the block until he knew for sure that she was in for the night—or not. Maybe he'd just go to her door and forget the sneaky tactics. Dammit, he'd seen too much bad stuff in the past few years. Hard as he tried, he couldn't write off Sara's recent troubles as nothing of concern, not without knowing more.

Sara dressed for her walk, then sat in the foyer and placed her hands in her lap. She was not a coward. She would not become a coward. And still, she couldn't help but remember how anxious she'd felt last night when she hadn't known Dante was following her. What if the man who'd stolen her underwear and replaced it with teeny slips of colorful silk was out there right now, watching? What if he had been watching for weeks or months? She shuddered.

She'd never minded living alone. She missed Robert, of course—she'd cried for his loss for a long time. But she'd never been afraid to be alone, to make her own way, to live in this big house on her own. Not until now.

Some days she thought it wasn't fair that she had lost so much. Her mother when she was just four; her father not long after she'd turned twelve. She'd had her grandfather, her beloved Papa, of course, and had never felt unloved or abandoned, but now even he was gone. Grandparents, parents, Robert...

When the doorbell rang, she nearly jumped out of her skin. She sprang toward the door and peeked through the glass panel beside it, pulling back the fabric that offered some gauzy privacy. She almost melted in relief when she saw Dante standing there. No suit tonight. He was dressed in a T-shirt and longish shorts and running shoes. There was also no gun, not that she could see.

She opened the door.

"You're late," he said simply.

"For what?"

"You said you walk at the same time every evening, so you're late."

"I was thinking of skipping my walk tonight," she confessed.

He took in her attire—tennis shoes and shorts and T-shirt—and lifted his eyebrows.

"All right," she confessed, "I was sitting here about to chicken out. I wondered if the sicko who left that underwear on my porch might be watching. If that makes me a coward, then so be it."

"It makes you smart. Cautious," he added. "There's nothing wrong with that." And then he grinned. "Besides, I'm here to keep you company on your walk. I need a bit of exercise myself."

She doubted her idea of exercise would raise so much as a bead of sweat on his body, but she didn't argue. "I'll grab my house keys."

Yesterday she had been a bit stunned by Dante's presence on her doorstep and in her usually staid life. Tonight as they walked she was more comfortable. She didn't wonder if anyone was watching. She didn't care. They talked about Tillman and how it had changed in recent years, and they talked about Jesse and his family—mostly the kids. Sara felt a bitter pang as they talked about the newest addition to the family, little Olivia. She'd wanted children, at least one child, but Robert had convinced her that they had plenty of time. As an assistant D.A. he worked such long hours, he hadn't thought it would be fair to her to bring a child into the world when he wasn't home more to be a proper father. When he went into private practice, the time would be better. They had years to plan their family. He'd been wrong, and now here she was, thirty-five years old, alone, burying herself in politics and charities to make the days fly past.

Suddenly it seemed she didn't want the days to fly past. What was she missing by hiding so much of herself away? Was it really too late?

"Do you have children?" she asked, trying to make the question sound casual and meaningless.

Dante reacted quickly and with decisiveness. "No. Not my thing."

He said it wasn't his "thing," but Dante would be a protective father, she imagined. Maybe he wouldn't be involved in Little League and school activities the way his cousin was, but he wouldn't be neglectful or uncaring. He had taken to protecting her quite easily. She could only imagine how he would be with a child.

She'd be a wonderful mother, if only she had the chance....

Tick, tock. Tick, tock. She wasn't getting any younger. Sara squirmed in her own skin. Was she hiding here in Tillman where she felt safe? Was she so afraid of losing again that she'd shut down her hopes and desires? She hadn't been so acutely aware of her ticking biological clock until Dante had appeared on her doorstep. Coincidence? Unlikely. *Very* unlikely.

"Let me make you dinner," she said as her house came into view.

"Thanks, but that's not necessary."

"I know it's not *necessary.*" She stopped where the sidewalk met the walkway to her front door. For a moment she looked into his eyes, not flinching at the power she saw there, not ignoring the potent pull that had not diminished in eighteen years. No wonder she had fallen into his arms so easily, all those years ago. No wonder she had gotten lost in his kiss. Even now, their chemistry was explosive. She'd never known anything like it. "I want you to stay. I want to talk. I'd like to know what your life has been like since I saw you last." Would it be too telling to admit that she was tired of eating alone almost every night? Would it be too forward to admit that she simply didn't want him to go? "Providing a meal is the least I can do to thank you for keeping me company so I can walk in peace."

Dante did hesitate, but not for long. "Sure. Why not?"

He shouldn't be here. Sitting in Sara's kitchen watching her cook and listening to her talk seemed to pull at him, as if she were drawing him into her life one tiny bit at a time. She was a woman now, not a girl, but her movements and the tone of her voice were familiar enough to make that pull seem easy and natural.

She'd kicked off her shoes but still wore the clothes she'd walked in. So did he. It wasn't like their "exercise" had been vigorous enough to work up a sweat. Sara's evening walk had been nothing more than a warm-up for him, and a nice long run sounded pretty good about now. Would a run work off some of this nervous energy? Would running until his body hurt help him get his brain back on track?

He doubted it would help much, or for very long. His eyes were drawn to Sara, and it didn't take him long to quit fighting his instincts and look to his heart's content. The shorts she wore hugged her hips and the T-shirt that advertised a local restaurant was stretched over yet another sturdy bra. Her hair was arranged simply, pulled away from her perfectly sculptured face. She didn't look like any mayor he had ever seen before, that's for sure.

She threw some vegetables into a wok. They sizzled, she stirred, and then she turned to face him. "You said you're staying in a duplex?"

"Yeah. It's just about three blocks away. On Conyer Street."

"Patty used to live over there, before she got married."

"Your friend," he said, remembering the brunette from that morning.

"Yes. Why aren't you staying with Jesse?" Spatula in hand, she crossed her arms and wagged the utensil in his direction.

"I did, for a few days." He shook his head. "With all those kids running everywhere, it's chaos all the time. Early in the morning, middle of the night, any and all hours of the day. Chaos."

Her smile grew wider. "'All those kids'? They have three children, and whenever I've seen them, they've been very well behaved."

"Then *you* live with them," he said, only a little bit sour. When a kid threw himself into Dante's bed at six-thirty in the morning, the results were not pretty. He'd come damn near to instinctively throwing Ethan across the room on his second morning in the Edwards household.

Sara turned around and stirred, and for a moment Dante allowed his gaze to rest on the rounded wonderfulness of her ass. His hands itched to reach out and touch. An ache and a twitch settled in low, telling him in a primitive way how he wanted Sara. Where the hell was this going? Like it or not, it was sure as hell going somewhere. Would she allow it? Did she itch and ache? There was only one way to find out.

He left his chair and in three long strides was behind Sara. She knew he was there, he could tell by the tension in her body and the way she held her breath. He placed his hands on her waist and leaned in and down, pressing his lips to her neck, feeling a rush of relief and excitement that he did not even attempt to restrain. She was warm and soft and yielding, and in this moment she was his.

She didn't tell him to stop; didn't squirm and move out of his reach. No, she stood very still until she tilted her head to one side to give him greater access. Yes, she was *his*.

Sara tasted good. She tasted of soap and sweat and woman. He flicked his tongue against her skin and let his hands drop so he was holding her hips. His mouth lingered on the flesh beneath her ear, and he felt the tremble that passed through her entire body.

He was hard and more than willing and she was dancing on the edge. One push, and she'd go flying beyond and over that edge. One touch; one word.

But Dante was acutely aware that they were no better suited than they'd been as teenagers. Sara was vulnerable at the moment and he could, with very little effort, get what he had not been able to get from her all those years ago. Everything. The right touch, the right words, and he'd be inside her. It was what he wanted, what he needed.

He dropped his hands and took a half step back. "The stir-fry's burning," he said, his voice unexpectedly gruff.

Sara began to stir with a renewed vigor. She did not turn to look at him. "So it is," she whispered.

Just like before, what he wanted and needed and what was right for her was not the same. Nowhere close. Some things never changed.

"I'm not staying for dinner," he said.

Now she turned around, spun, actually, to glare at him. "What? It's almost finished."

This wasn't about supper, and they both knew it. He took her chin in his hand and looked into her eyes. Damn, there was so much there. Emotion, intelligence, questions, hopes. "Maybe I haven't seen you in a lifetime, Sarabeth, but I know what you want and I'm not that man."

"You don't have any idea what I want," she protested. He was glad she didn't play the coy, "I have no idea what you're talking about" card. She didn't brush him off and pretend that she wasn't caught up in the same physical attraction that had come out of the blue and knocked him sideways.

"I saw the look in your eyes when I was talking about Jesse's kids and the chaos that comes with them. That's what you want. You want a home and a family and a forever man. That's not me."

"Maybe not," she said sharply, "but you're here now and I like you and I think you like me well enough."

She hadn't been interested in temporary as a teenager, and he had a hard time believing she'd settle for it now. "I like you well enough," he confessed. "Too much, maybe."

"If you liked me less, you'd stay?"

"Maybe."

"Then like me less." She moved up and brought her mouth to his, and she kissed him.

Sara's lips were so soft, so perfect for his own, that with one touch he felt as if he were falling into her. Her lips parted slightly, and there he was…falling, captured, wanting nothing more than to stay attached to this woman who wanted everything he was not. He wanted her bare skin against his, he wanted her naked body wrapped around his.

He flicked his tongue into her mouth, just barely, and she grounded herself by placing her hands on his waist.

Some things never changed. Whatever had drawn them together eighteen years ago was still there, and it was as real and powerful as ever.

He broke the kiss and leaned past her to turn off the stove. The stir-fry was now burned beyond repair. "I hope you have a TV dinner in the freezer."

"I do."

"You're going to need it." He kissed her once more, quickly this time, and then he stepped away and turned his attention to business. His business: the business of trouble. "I noticed that you have a security system. Do you arm it every night?"

Sara blinked twice, obviously surprised by the abrupt way he'd changed the subject. "Most nights."

"Until this is settled, I want you to make sure it's on whenever you're here alone, got it?"

"Yes, but..."

"No buts. Day and night, if you're here alone I want the system armed."

"Okay," she said softly.

"Do you have a gun?"

"No!" She sounded horrified by the prospect.

"We'll take care of that ASAP. Until then..."

"How can you kiss me like that and then start talking about guns and alarms?" Her frustration was evident, not only in the tone of her voice but in the fierce set of her mouth and the fire in her eyes.

"I told you, I'm not what you're looking for, Sara."

"Maybe you should let me be the judge of that. I'm a grown woman now, Dante. I'm perfectly capable of knowing what I want and what I don't want."

She wasn't going to make this easy. "Fine. This has nothing to do with you and what you want. You're not what *I* need. I don't need the complications of a relationship, even a one-nighter, with a needy woman. I don't want you."

Sara looked as if he'd slapped her, and he felt instantly guilty. If she was paying very close attention to his body's reactions, she knew that last statement wasn't at all true. Unfortunately for both of them, the rest of his arguments were dead on.

* * *

So much for her efforts at being forward and available. She'd invited Dante into her house and made small talk. She'd smiled and flirted—a little—and asked all the appropriate questions about his life. She'd been prepared to feed him, trying to make her way to his heart—or whatever body part she might be able to claim—through his stomach.

She had never imagined that he didn't want her. After that kiss she still wasn't sure that was the case. He'd kissed and touched and looked like a man who wanted her plenty. How could such powerful chemistry be one-sided? Surely he felt *something!*

But the hard truth was, he was gone and she was alone, security alarm armed, television on, the work she'd brought home neglected.

Not all that much different from last time they'd parted, she thought bitterly as she headed for bed.

Was he right? Had her sudden thoughts of babies made her all but throw herself at him? Did she, somewhere in the back of her mind, think of Dante as more than a potential short-lived fling? No. He did something to her, physically and emotionally. She simply wanted to explore that *something,* even if it wasn't meant to last. She wanted to laugh again, to feel again, to get lost in pleasure again. She didn't care how long he might or might not stay.

Who was she kidding? She didn't fling. She never had. Dante was right. Dammit. If they ended up in bed together, she'd fall in love with him all over again, and even though she was a big girl now, it would still hurt when he left—as he surely would.

She really should give in and let Lydia set her up on that blind date she'd been going on about for the past three months. Lydia's insurance salesman had divorced last year and was available. And lonely. And very sweet. He was not a handsome man, Lydia said, but he was far from ugly. Apparently he had seen Sara around town, at various functions, and was "interested." If all she wanted was a reawakening of her physical self, wouldn't someone like that do as well as Dante? It might be even better because her expectations would be so very low.

Like it or not, she wanted more than a loveless relationship built on low expectations. After her years of mourning, after living through a time when she'd believed her life as a woman who was able to love was over and done, she had begun to have hope once again. Maybe there was another man out there for her, someone who wanted a home and children and a best friend. Someone who would love her. Someone who would make her laugh again.

Long past her usual bedtime, lying in bed in the dark, Sara couldn't sleep. Dante's Crown Vic was not parked outside her window tonight, and she found she missed his possessive presence. She didn't want to sleep. She was afraid she'd dream of dark-haired babies and wake up crying for everything she'd missed. She was afraid some sick pervert would be sitting out there on her street where Dante was not, ready and willing to fling skimpy underwear at her house or to steal something else so very personal.

What had the thief done with the bras and panties he'd taken from her clothesline? She shuddered. She didn't want to know.

A noise that seemed to come from directly beneath her window made her sit up straight. She tried not to let fear consume her as she strained to hear more clearly. What she'd heard might have been a dog or a cat roaming the neighborhood, but she couldn't be sure and given the recent events it seemed prudent to look.

Sara eased herself from the bed even though she knew nothing—or no one—would hear her movements from outside the house. After tiptoeing across the room, she very gently parted the lace curtains at her bedroom window and glanced down. There were well-trimmed shrubberies beneath her window, and from this vantage point it seemed that one of them was misshapen.

Suddenly the shape moved, and she realized that there was a man crouched by her shrubs.

Her heart beat too hard and she lost her breath as she ran to the wingback chair where she'd tossed her purse earlier in the evening. She worked the clasp with trembling fingers, opening the small leather bag and grabbing for the business card Dante had give her earlier in the day. With the card in hand she snagged her bedside phone and dialed his cell number, and as she did a new noise caught her attention.

Whoever was standing beneath her window began throwing pebbles at the panes, small pebbles that sounded like sleet against the glass. Between one assault and the next she was quite sure that in spite of all the barriers between them, in spite of the glass and the brick and the alarm system, she heard him call her name.

Sarabeth.

Dante answered before the second ring, and when

she heard his voice she was washed in comfort and relief, and in that instant she knew that her new sense of coming back to life had nothing to do with time or biological clocks. It was Dante who called to her, and no blind date would ever be able to take his place.

Chapter 4

Dante hadn't been asleep or anywhere near sleep when Sara called his cell. He'd been sitting in front of a crappy old television that came with the duplex, watching an action/comedy movie he'd seen a dozen times. His mind had been restless since coming to Tillman, and sitting in front of the flickering television he'd been thinking of a reason—or an excuse—to leave. It wasn't as if Jesse asked for a lot of favors, but Dante could argue that he'd come when asked, like a good relative should. There had been a couple of new hires, which left the department in slightly better shape than it had been when he'd arrived, so it wasn't as if he would be deserting a sinking ship.

It hadn't taken three minutes to get to Sara's house. She'd been waiting for him in the foyer and threw the front door open wide when she saw him coming up her walk. Dante assured himself she was all right, then he instructed her to lock the door and wait while he checked the perimeter of the house, searching for the trespasser she'd claimed to see.

The yard was quiet. Deserted. Peaceful, the way late night in a small town could be. There was no sign of the man she'd claimed had stood outside her bedroom and called her name, although Dante told himself he would check again, after the sun was up. Her outdoor lights were bright, but they left too many shadows for him to be certain he'd seen all there was to see. If she were a different sort of woman he might think she'd lied just to get him over there, but she wasn't that kind of woman, and she was too obviously scared. She wasn't that good an actress.

When he returned to the house he found an anxious Sara in the foyer. Again, she opened the door just as he reached it. She was wide-eyed and trembling, shaken to the bone by the fright of seeing—or imagining—a man beneath her window. No, she wasn't acting. Dante put aside any and all thoughts of leaving Tillman.

He wasn't sure what kind of nightwear she had on beneath the plain white robe, but it wasn't the heavy flannel pajamas he had imagined. There was *no* drawstring. Beneath the robe's hem her very nice legs were bare. A hint of white lace peeking out from the collar also hinted that she didn't sleep naked. Too bad.

"Did you find anything?" she asked.

Either whoever had been beneath her window had left without leaving any physical signs of his presence, or Sara had been so wound up she'd imagined the whole thing. Or dreamed it. Dante didn't think she'd accept that theory, so he didn't bother. He shook his head. "Nothing. I'll check again in the morning, just to be sure."

She closed the door and set the alarm with trembling fingers. Dante didn't tell her to wait until he'd left to set the security system, because even though he hadn't found any signs of trouble he wasn't going anywhere.

Wasn't this a fine state of affairs? Just as he'd convinced himself to back off for both their sakes, this happened. Maybe if he could make himself think of Sara as a client, it would be easier. He'd shared houses and apartments and even hotel rooms with scared, lonely women who needed protection, and even when they'd thrown themselves at him—because they were scared or lonely or horny or all three—he'd managed to remain professional, to keep his distance.

Then again, pretty as those women had been, he hadn't wanted any one of them the way he wanted Sara.

"Do you have a spare bedroom?" he asked.

She looked a little suspicious but was definitely more relieved than alarmed by his question. "Several. Take your pick."

There didn't seem to be any question about the matter. He was moving in.

By the time Sara woke in the morning, after a restless night spent as much awake as asleep, she'd convinced herself that she hadn't seen or heard anything last night. So why was she still soothed to know that Dante slept down the hall?

Smelling the coffee and bacon and realizing with a start that Opal had arrived, Sara bounded out of bed.

How was she going to explain Dante to the older woman? Opal Greenwood had worked for Robert's family for years, first as a housekeeper, then as a cook, then as assistant to Robert's father. These days the woman, who was in her midfifties but appeared much younger, did a little bit of everything. Sara was perfectly capable of doing all the jobs Opal did for her herself, but it was nice to have help, especially when it came to cleaning this big house and handling the correspondence related to the charities the Vance and Caldwell families had been involved with for many years.

Opal had been dedicated to Robert and to his father, and she was openly protective of Sara's position as the last living Vance in Tillman.

Sara rushed through her shower and styled her hair simply, pulling it up and back. A two-minute application of makeup followed. She grabbed the closest suitable outfit from her closet. The gray pantsuit was not exciting, but it was comfortable and it fit well enough, and the fall of the jacket made her look almost flat-chested. No man would ever look at her twice while she was wearing this outfit. That had been the point, hadn't it?

She stepped into her most comfortable shoes, and then she all but ran down the stairs so she could explain to Opal what was going on before Dante made an appearance.

Before she reached the kitchen, she knew she was too late. She couldn't understand the words, but the low timbre of his voice was unmistakable. Whatever Dante said was followed by a few curt words from Opal.

Great. They'd met.

Sara put on a smile as she joined them. Opal was

busy at the stove. Dante sat at the small kitchen table, sipping on a cup of coffee.

There was a large, finely furnished dining room a few steps away, but it was rarely used. Sara had always preferred the kitchen table. This room was much warmer than the formal dining area, more like home. She hadn't moved here until months after Robert's death, so she had never entertained or held family celebrations here, as she might have if they'd lived in Tillman after their marriage.

Sara had put her stamp on a few rooms in this old house, and the kitchen was one of them. She had gotten rid of the dark table that had once taken up so much of the space and replaced it with a smaller round one in oak, and she'd had the cabinets painted white. She'd put the old everyday china in storage and bought bright, colorful dishware and mugs. Opal had not liked the changes at all, but then she'd worked there for a long time and was accustomed to things as they had once been.

Nothing was as it had once been. Sara knew that too well.

That morning Dante's back was to the kitchen window. It was a seat chosen, she imagined, so he could see everything that was going on in the large kitchen. His eyes fell on her as she entered the room, and he smiled tightly.

"Good morning," he said. "Did you sleep well?"

Opal, who did not even turn around to look at her, made a low grunting noise.

"Not all that well, I'm afraid. I do thank you for coming over when I called last night," she said, hoping to kill two birds with one stone—thank Dante and explain to Opal. "I was so scared by the noises, but this morning I wonder if I actually heard anything at all."

"I checked under your window this morning," Dante said with a touch of obvious annoyance. "By the light of day there does appear to be some small amount of disturbance there."

Her heart dropped into her stomach. Just when she'd been about to convince herself that there was nothing to worry about...

"I didn't find anything worth analyzing, I'm afraid," Dante continued.

Now Opal looked at her, and instead of being annoyed the older woman looked concerned. "Did you have a fright last night? My goodness, that's just terrible. I wondered why the alarm was set when I came in."

Dante glared at Sara. "You told me you set the alarm at night," he said accusingly.

"I sometimes do," Sara said.

"You're here alone, you should be setting it every night." He sounded annoyed. "Does anyone besides Opal have the code?" Again he looked as if he were accusing her of something. Surely he didn't think there was anything wrong with her only personal employee having the code. Since the older woman was usually there before Sara got out of bed, it was only practical.

"I don't think so."

"You don't *think?*"

Sara gave him a glare of her own. "I need caffeine before we continue this conversation." She retrieved her favorite bright pink mug and poured herself a cup of coffee, taking her time so she could regain her composure. If the ground beneath her window had been slightly disturbed, did that mean someone really had been there, throwing pebbles at her window and whispering her name? She shuddered. She hadn't known being mayor of a small town would come with stalkers. After all, this was Tillman, not Atlanta or New York. She knew almost everyone in town. There were still people who didn't even bother to lock their doors at night, much less set alarms. The concerns here were simple ones. There was no reason for a man to haunt her, to harass and frighten her.

Of course, the underwear stolen and the resulting "gift" hinted that her stalker's concern was not political or financial in nature.

"What now?" she asked as she turned around to face Dante, warm mug in hand.

"I'm not sure," he said softly. "I would say I could move in until we know for sure what's going on, but this is Tillman, and I do remember how tongues can wag."

She couldn't help but think of seeing Dante at this table every morning, of speaking to him before going to bed every night. The response that rushed through her was warm and comforting and, yes, even exhilarating. She wanted him there more than she'd wanted anything for a very long time. "I don't care about gossip," she said.

Again, Opal made that soft grunting noise that spoke so clearly of disapproval.

"Be very sure about that," Dante said softly.

Sara hesitated a moment, and then she nodded her head once.

Opal efficiently placed two plates filled with eggs, bacon and grits on the kitchen table. "I need to take care of some correspondence this morning," she said crisply. "Before I leave for the day please let me know if you're going to change the code on the burglar alarm." She glared at Dante. "If you want to keep the code a secret from a woman who's run this household for more than thirty years, then from now on you can make your own damned breakfast."

The comment and the anger were directed toward Dante, not Sara. No, Opal wasn't angry at her employer. What Sara saw in those eyes, when they were turned to her, was pure disappointment.

Opal had loved Robert. Maybe she didn't want to see him replaced. Still, Sara had politely fended off many phone calls and invitations and even unexpected gentlemen callers, especially in the past two years, and Opal had never shown even the smallest amount of annoyance at the appearance or interest of a man. She'd even encouraged Sara to see her own son, Elliott, and had arranged for them to have dinner together more than once. It hadn't taken Sara any time at all to realize that she and Elliott had nothing in common. Nothing at all.

So Opal was obviously not opposed to Sara having a man in her life, but right now she was livid because a strange man was sitting at the kitchen table. Maybe it had just been a shock for her to arrive this morning and find a man in the kitchen.

No, it was something else, something more than surprise. Somehow Opal saw what Sara saw, that Dante was different, that he *could be* very different. Did the older woman still hold out hope that Sara and Elliott would get together? Did Opal want her only child and the only remaining member of the family she'd served all her adult life to merge into one? That would never happen. Elliott wasn't all that bright, and he was easily distracted. His mind had wandered often during their few uncomfortable dinners.

Then again, Dante hadn't bothered to tell Opal that he didn't want Sara, not in any way. She had no reason to worry.

"So," Sara said as she pushed grits around with her fork, "what happens next?"

"We have a couple of options." Dante took a bite of his eggs and chewed while he pondered those options. The eggs were followed by a bite of bacon and a swig of coffee. "I can move in, so you won't be here alone at night. The arrangement would be strictly professional, of course."

"Of course," she repeated, though the reaction of her heart was anything but professional.

"We can set up a detail of Tillman officers to patrol the house every hour or so, night and day. Their appearance alone might scare this guy off. I can call a couple of friends and a couple of favors and put you under twenty-four-hour guard." His eyes met and held hers. "Or we can do all three."

"All three? Isn't that a bit excessive?"

"Maybe," he said. "Maybe not." He picked up a piece of crisp bacon and took a bite, then rolled his eyes. "Man, this is a good breakfast. I was getting so tired of Pop-Tarts."

"Grown men don't eat Pop-Tarts."

He grinned at her. "Yes, they do. Frosted blueberry has gotten me through a lot of jobs."

Sara found herself smiling. "If you move in, Opal's cooking will be one of the benefits."

"No more burnt stir-fry?" he teased.

She blushed at the memory. "I do occasionally cook for myself, but more often than not Opal leaves something in the fridge and all I have to do is heat it up. It all depends on how much other work she has during the day and whether or not she has plans that evening."

"You're not afraid she'll try to poison my food?" he joked. The housekeeper's anger had not gone unnoticed.

"She'll come around." Surely once Sara explained about the anonymous underwear and how much the noises outside her window had scared her, Opal would understand. Surely. "For now, let's handle it this way: you move in, in a professional capacity as you said, and we get available officers to drive by the house now and then. Not every hour, that would be too much of a burden, but when they're in the area and have the time, they can make a loop around the block." Maybe, as he said, that would scare her problem away.

Dante nodded in agreement, and Sara returned her attention to her breakfast, certain that the man sitting at her kitchen table would turn out to be more trouble than any panty thief.

Sara had underestimated how having Dante living under the same roof would strain her to the breaking point. He hadn't been there an entire twenty-four hours yet, and she'd spent many of those hours at city hall buried in work, and still, she felt so on edge she was about to pop.

She never popped. Not anymore. She had become what she was expected to be. Staid, responsible, professional, well-mannered—unpoppable.

Tonight he had walked with her again, and they'd talked about inconsequential matters. The weather had been a very popular subject before they had finally given up and just walked in silence. With every step, her anxiety had increased. Did Dante feel that anxiety, too, or was he always wound so tight when he was on the job?

Opal had left a chicken casserole in the fridge, and when the walk was over, they put the casserole in the oven and she made a fresh pitcher of sweet iced tea. Dante made sure the alarm was set and all the doors and windows were securely locked, and then he sat in the kitchen with her and waited for their supper to be finished.

Sara knew she could do them both a favor and retire to her room right after supper, but she didn't think she'd take that cowardly route. Dante's presence made her think more than she should. Not only think, but *feel*. Yes, lately she'd been feeling much more than was proper. Seeing him sitting in her kitchen made her question her decisions, her priorities, her life.

If she thought grabbing him and kissing him again would get him into her bed, she'd do it in a heartbeat. She was not normally a bold woman. She was never bold! But Dante made her want to be what she was not. He made her want to face life. To *take* it. After all, she was a grown woman, not a child who needed to be told what was good for her and what was not.

She knew damn well Dante Mangino wasn't good for her, and she still wanted him. The problem was, she wasn't the kind of woman who would attempt to take what she wanted if it meant getting hurt. He'd already told her once that he didn't want her. She knew he wasn't here to stay. That should be enough for any woman.

When the casserole was finished cooking, she poured two glasses of tea and he got down the plates. There was fruit salad in the fridge, and he got that out and put the yellow bowl on the table. They didn't speak as dinner was prepared, but there was a strange kind of comfort in their companionship. She usually ate alone. Did he? She usually ate in front of the television, the only sounds the fake conversations of actors or the solemn delivery of news by anchormen. Did he?

When they sat down at the table and she looked him in the eye across the table, she felt a shimmer of something she could not explain away. It was physical and more. It was wanting mixed with fear. Fear of rejection. Fear of getting it wrong. Fear of losing again.

Fear was costing her what was left of her life. What did she really have to lose at this point?

She smiled. He did not.

"Opal's really a good cook," she said, stirring the hot casserole on her plate.

"There are vegetables in here," Dante complained. "This isn't, like, health food, is it?"

Sara laughed, and that made Dante's eyes snap up to meet hers.

"Is there anything wrong with health food?" she asked.

"Yeah, it tastes like cardboard."

She could disagree, but instead she just said, "You can rest easy. Opal uses enough fat in all her recipes to make sure nothing qualifies as health food."

The weather and now food. If she was going to take a chance and try to draw Dante into her life, even if just for a while, then their conversations were going to have to get more personal. "I can't believe you never married. Isn't there even an ex-Mrs. Mangino out there somewhere?"

"No." He squirmed, at least a little uncomfortable. "Tell me about your husband," he said. Maybe he thought turning the subject to her late husband would put some distance between them.

What he didn't know was that talking about Robert only made her miss their companionship, their laughter, their private moments.

"He was a lawyer."

"Oh, can I make nasty lawyer jokes?" Dante asked. "Please?"

Sara laughed. "Go right ahead. Robert did it all the time."

"If you give me permission, it's not nearly as much fun."

Sara felt like a bit of a wall had come tumbling down. Maybe that wall was just cracked a little. "He was an assistant district attorney in Atlanta."

"A good guy, eh?" Dante said.

"Yeah." And then he'd gotten sick and died, an inch at a time. She didn't want that to be a part of the conversation. Maybe she was healing at last, but she wasn't entirely numb to the painful memories. "Sounds as if you do good-guy work yourself."

"Sometimes."

It was a little like pulling teeth, but eventually Dante did relax as he talked about his job and the men he had worked with for so many years. She was horrified to hear that he'd been shot once, although he told the story as if revealing that he'd once skinned a knee.

And then, as they finished their meal and drained the last of the glass of tea, he looked her in the eye and she saw something that reminded her very much of what she was feeling at the moment. He might say he didn't want her, but that was a lie. He didn't want to want her; that was another matter entirely. How much could she ask for? How hard could she push? She wanted Dante in her life for as long as he would stay, and she was terrified that if she let him walk away, she'd slip back into oblivion, where she was nothing more than what other people expected her to be.

The past couple of days had been quiet, so much so that Dante questioned the wisdom of moving into Sara's house. It wasn't as if he needed to see her more often, to share close quarters, to have dinner and breakfast and share coffee and talk about the weather in order to fill the occasional awkward silence. To want her and not be able to have her, to know that there were no two people on the planet less well suited to one another in every possible way. Except the physical. He had a feeling they'd be very well suited in that department. It would not be wise to explore that feeling.

If the weekend remained quiet, he would probably move out on Monday. Not that he wouldn't check on her often, and the frequent patrols would continue for some time, but, dammit, he was in serious need of some time away from Mayor Sara Vance. The woman got under his skin in a big way.

This was the worst. He'd never been to a sock burning before, and had followed along with no idea what to expect. A bonfire burned in a clearing a safe distance from a picturesque white farmhouse. The burn area was surrounded by rocks of many sizes. This was no campfire set by kids but a well-planned and safe blaze. They'd done this before, that was obvious.

Before the actual ritual, there were hot dogs and marshmallows to be toasted over the fire. Someone had a portable stereo, and modern country music that sounded almost like southern rock played softly, drifting through the pleasant night air. Lydia and Patty and their respective spouses were present, as were a handful of little kids. He wasn't sure which kids belonged to whom and didn't really care.

The brunette, Patty, he'd met briefly at city hall on Wednesday morning. She looked different in worn jeans and a T-shirt but smiled just as wickedly. Lydia, who was at least a couple of inches shorter than the other two women and had a wild mass of curly light brown hair, was mother to at least three of the rug rats who were running around the place. Her smile was softer but no less genuine.

The white farmhouse where Lydia and her brood lived was not so far from the bonfire that there weren't frequent trips to the bathroom or to fetch favorite toys and more ice. Still, beneath the stars and beside the fire they were isolated. The gathering felt almost primitive.

Sara's friends' husbands were two normal nice guys who drank beer and talked about football even though the season was over—or months away, depending on which way you wanted to figure it. Of course, this was Alabama, and football was always a proper subject of conversation. Because Dante was Jesse's cousin he wasn't considered a stranger, and even though his eyes rarely left Sara, he participated in the conversation with real interest.

He was apparently of great interest to Patty and Lydia. They stared. They smiled. They poked one another in the ribs and giggled when they thought he wasn't paying attention. Okay, he got it. It was long past time for Sara to get on with her life, long past time for her to allow another man in her life. She had explained to her friends that Dante was around because there was some minor concern over whoever had left the underwear on her porch, but they didn't quite buy it. They knew her too well.

Did they know that he had come so close to being her first that he could still almost taste it? Did they know that, like it or not, there was something between them that simply would not die? Did they know he'd kissed her? More rightly, she'd kissed him.

Maybe if she hadn't kissed him three days ago, he wouldn't be hard right now. Maybe if he didn't know too well how she smelled, how she fell into him when she kissed, how very warm she was, he wouldn't think almost constantly of making the short trip down the hall at night and crawling into her bed. Maybe he wouldn't fantasize about what she wore under that shapeless white robe. Maybe.

Finally the time came for the women to begin their spring ritual. They gathered their small bags of mismatched and holey socks and one by one tossed them into the fire. Usually the disposal was silent, but now and then they would add a tidbit of interest. "I wore these to the Christmas parade." "My mother gave me these." "The kids made a sock puppet out of the mate of this one." Not all the socks had stories attached, but a few did. The women laughed, they tossed the old socks one at a time into the fire and watched them get eaten away by the flames.

Until there was one woman and one sock left.

Sara looked down at the sock in her hand. It was difficult to see the details in the odd flickering light, but there was some sort of design on the single sock. He would never think of Sara has a funny-sock kind of girl, but she held on to the sock too tightly, as if she didn't want to let it go.

"Robert gave me these socks for Easter the year before he died. They have little chickens and pastel-colored eggs all over them." She laughed briefly and softly. "They're hideous. I told him so when he gave them to me. I haven't been able to find the mate to this sock for two years." Although it was ugly and mateless, she clutched the sock tightly for a moment.

The kids had wound down, all of them exhausted by the evening's fun, and the adults—Patty and Lydia especially—had turned somber. A night once filled with laughter and the screams of children grew heavily silent.

Sara looked down at the little sock. She squeezed the funny fabric once more and then she tossed it into the fire.

And suddenly Dante got it. This spring ritual wasn't just about getting rid of mismatched and ruined socks, it was about letting go. Of things, of the past, of pain, of all those things we sometimes hold on to for much too long. It was about moving on, embracing the present and the future and leaving behind what once had been.

Made him wish he'd brought along something to burn.

The others began to gather the children and all the paraphernalia that came with them. There was a round of good-nights and a few hugs. The socks had been properly burned, the evening was over. Lydia's husband had everything waiting close by that he needed to put out the fire. A bucket of water, a bucket of sand.

Sara turned to look at Dante, and like it or not he could see the mix of emotions on her face. She was relieved and sad, invigorated and serene. This was a big moment for her, he knew. How big a part of this moment was he? If he hadn't come to Tillman, if he wasn't living in her house, if they hadn't kissed, would she still have burned that sock tonight? Or would it have sat in a neatly arranged drawer for another year or two or ten?

She walked toward him, and almost without thought he reached for her hand. She took it. "I'm ready to go home," she said. "How about you?"

Dante wondered if Sara still bought the lie that he didn't want her. Judging by the easy way she held his hand as they walked toward his car, probably not.

When they reached the Crown Vic, he didn't immediately open the door for her but instead placed her there with her back against the passenger door and window and trapped her with his arms. He wouldn't be less than honest with her. "I'm not going to stay," he said bluntly.

"I know," she whispered.

"I'm not going to change my life or who I am, not for you or anyone else."

"I wouldn't ask you to."

"We're just two unattached adults looking for a little fun. That's it."

"If you say so." She grabbed his belt with one hand and held on.

"Nothing is going to…"

Sara interrupted him with a laugh and a, "Dammit, Dante, why don't you just shut up and kiss me?"

He did, leaning in and placing his mouth on hers, taking that kiss without reservation. Without a single doubt. She tugged on his belt. He slipped his hand just beneath her T-shirt to rest on her warm side. She had a woman's skin, soft and warm. Her lips parted, her head tilted, and he was lost.

He was lost in the kiss, and still, in the back of his mind, he was warned by a whispered *You never should've come back.* He wanted more; he wanted all of her, and still, he knew they were wrong for each other.

Wrong in every way but this one. He couldn't remember the last time he had wanted a woman so much. They were adults and she knew his intentions were far from honorable, so why should he stop?

Dante reluctantly took his mouth from hers and opened the passenger door. "Done so soon?" she asked as she slid inside and took her seat.

"I'm too old for sex in the backseat," he said, not feeling the need to explain that a few more minutes and that's where they'd be, mostly naked and contorted in the backseat of another one of Jesse's cars. His hand up her shirt, her hand timidly exploring, their sweat mingling.

Only this time, there would be no stopping.

Chapter 5

Sara was restless, as Dante drove silently to her house. He did want her, and she was ready. Ready to let go of the past and take a chance, ready to step out of her well-controlled comfort zone to take a risk. The biggest risk of all. Maybe she wasn't exactly laying her heart on the line, but offering her body was almost the same thing. She didn't do sex without emotion, without thought and commitment.

She felt as if her body and heart had been sleeping for years, and Dante had awakened them both the moment he'd appeared on her doorstep. He said he wouldn't stay, and she believed him. She knew he did not require the same sort of emotion and commitment that she did for a sexual liaison. And she didn't care. Maybe in the morning she would have a second thought or two, but tonight she had none.

He parked in the driveway, since her car was in the one-car garage out back. By now the neighbors were probably accustomed to seeing the Crown Vic there. She truly didn't care. When she'd decided to weather whatever scandal Dante's presence caused, she had completely set aside any concerns about recriminations or disapproval. This was her life. Just because she was mayor, that didn't mean the town's residents had a right to comment on her private life, as well as her public service—not that having the right or not would stop them.

Dante had a key to her house and he had her front door unlocked and open by the time she reached it. He quickly punched the code into the security system. They were locked in then, alone and isolated, and nothing mattered but what they wanted and needed from each other.

As wordless as he had been on the drive home, Dante pulled her into his arms and kissed her again. The kiss was deeper this time, more demanding and more raw. He unsnapped and unzipped her blue jeans while they kissed, never missing a beat. His hands didn't tremble like hers did; he did not hesitate.

Sara felt as if she was caught in a whirlwind. The kiss took her breath away. Dante's fingers slipping inside her opened zipper made her body lurch. Nothing mattered but physical sensation and the burning need that threatened to swirl out of control.

Dante was heat and exhilaration—he was everything she was not. He was everything she had denied herself for so long. Her body had not forgotten what it was like to be caught up in passion. Her hips moved instinctively toward his, her lips and her tongue sought and held his kiss. Her body was drawn to his in an instinctive way, and in moments, her brain had ceased to function and she was operating entirely on impulse.

He broke the kiss and whipped her shirt over her head. He unfastened her bra with a too-practiced flick of his fingers and then discarded it. His mouth was there, on her throat and then on her breasts. She held on to his head and tilted her head back as he aroused her with his lips and his tongue. Her entire body trembled, her heart was in her throat, and she felt a rush of moisture…and they hadn't even moved three feet away from the front door yet.

"Here?" she asked breathlessly when Dante started to push her jeans over her hips.

He paused, and that was when she knew he'd been as caught up in the moment as she. "No," he said, his voice husky and sexy as hell. "I want you in a bed." He followed that statement with a soft kiss to her throat. "Your room or mine?"

"Yours," she whispered. "It's closer." Closer by a few feet, but at the moment that short distance seemed very important.

Dante surprised her by picking her up and carrying her. This was no romantic lift à la Scarlett O'Hara. Instead, he threw her over his shoulder.

Sara laughed as Dante ran up the stairs with her dangling from his shoulder, bouncing roughly with each bounding step. There were night-lights throughout the house, low-burning decorative lights that kept them from being in complete darkness. None burned in the guest room Dante had taken, however. There had been one there—a blue iris night-light—but he'd unplugged it and stuck it in a drawer so the nighttime illumination wouldn't ruin his night vision, he said. Still, with the door open there was a little bit of soft light drifting in from the hallway. She could see him, as he tossed her onto the bed. She could see him, as he lowered himself to hover above her.

She could see him until his mouth returned to hers and she closed her eyes so she could savor the sensations that whipped through her body.

At seventeen Dante had fumbled a bit—he'd lost his cool and moved too fast or too hard. Once they'd bumped foreheads, she remembered, and on one occasion he'd spent several awkward minutes trying to get her bra unsnapped.

That uncertain boy had been replaced by a man who did not fumble, who knew how and when. Sara felt as if she was on a roller-coaster. Her stomach had dropped out from under her; she wanted to scream. Even though she knew the big finish was the most exciting part of the trip, she did not want this ride to end.

Dante undressed her the rest of the way, getting rid of her shoes, her jeans, her panties. When he was finished she was entirely bare and totally vulnerable, lying across his bed waiting anxiously for him to come to her.

He kissed her again, and again, and this time she took the opportunity to caress him through strained jeans, to stroke him so he'd be in the same wonderful place she was.

"Don't want me?" she teased.

"I've always wanted you, you know that," he said gruffly.

"Yes, I know," she whispered.

He pulled off his shirt and then paused for a moment. "I don't suppose you're on the pill."

"No." She certainly hoped he didn't think he could *stop.*

"I have a condom." He reached for his wallet and pulled out a small packet, before discarding both the wallet and the jeans.

There was just enough light from the hallway for her to see his face well, as he lowered himself to her. He was so much sharper than he'd been as a boy, so much harder. The tattoos—one on his forearm, one on a bicep, one on his back and shoulder and neck—were new, at least to her. There were a number of scars on his once perfect body, scars that marked the years that had passed. But the eyes…the dark eyes she'd loved so well had not changed all that much. They still hinted at passion and depth and the heart he tried so hard to hide. She placed a hand on his cheek and shifted her hips to bring him closer. It was a mild night outdoors, but in here there was only heat. She was sweating; so was he. The very air she breathed seemed about to burst into flame.

And then he was inside her, and she could not think of anything else but the way their bodies came together. The way they moved, the way she needed all of him. Deeper, faster, and then she came hard, lifting her body from the bed, shaking and trembling as the intense pleasure shot through her.

Dante came with her, and cool as he seemed to be he, too, trembled. He, too, shook to his very core as he gave over to the connection of man to woman and the physical release it brought.

Sara closed her eyes and took a deep breath. Maybe this was wrong in some ways, but it was also very right.

She felt alive. She was awash in wonder. No other man but Dante could have brought her to this place.

"Would you think I was silly if I said I'd missed you?" she asked as he lay down beside her. It sounded foolish to her, but it didn't feel at all wrong.

"I would never accuse you of being silly," he whispered, one hand coming to rest on her belly, his lips finding and barely touching her shoulder. "Back in the day we didn't know each other all that well. Whatever it was we had didn't last long, and it's been a very long time," he said. "It's been a lifetime for both of us. But silly? Never."

She turned her head to study him. His body was hard and rippled with muscle. She studied the few stark tattoos and the scars. The tattoos seemed a part of him, and it wasn't as if he was covered in ink. The scars hurt her because she knew they'd hurt him.

He was teasing her with his words, but only a little. "I loved you," she said. The words seemed right when they were naked and happy. She was in a confessing mood, she supposed. "Maybe I loved you in the only way a young girl can love, before she knows what life's all about, but it was love."

"That's a word that gets tossed around a lot," he said, when a very simple *I used to love you, too,* would have sufficed quite nicely. There was no promise in "used to." No commitment in living in the past.

"Not by me," she said honestly. She wanted to ask him if he'd ever been in love, but she was terrified of the possible answers. "No" meant he was hopelessly broken. "Yes" meant he'd been in love with another woman. "You're right. That was a long time ago," she said, oddly comfortable stretched naked across Dante's bed. Oddly comfortable with the way he studied her bare body. It wasn't as if she didn't enjoy studying his, scars and all.

"Very long time."

"I used to wonder what my life would've been like if you'd stayed."

He grinned and winked at her. "Well, you wouldn't be mayor, that's for sure. I come with too many skeletons for a politician's closet." With that he left the bed to dispose of the condom and clean up a bit. Sara knew she really should return to her own bed for the night, but she didn't want to sleep alone. Unless Dante kicked her out, she was spending the night right here. She would hold him through the night, if he'd let her. She would touch him and kiss him and thank her lucky stars that he'd come back into her life.

He returned moments later with a warm, damp washcloth for her. And thank heavens, he did not kick her out of his bed.

Dante hadn't exactly been a monk for the past six years, so why did sleeping with Sara conjure up dreams about Serena? If he had to dream about her, why couldn't he remember the way she'd laughed, or the way she'd sometimes jumped him on the way to the gardener's shed or the way she'd kissed with total abandon? No, he had to dream about finding her dead in the same gardener's shed where they'd had sex so many times. Worse, in his dream she was not quite dead. She gurgled on her own blood. She looked him in the eye and told him it was *all his fault.*

As usual he apologized to her, again and again. It wasn't enough. Her eyes, eyes that stayed on him long after it was impossible for her to speak, did not forgive. He reached for her and his hands were covered in her blood. He tried to turn back time, since this was a dream and he knew it. Maybe he could save her this time, if he could only go back. But even in his dreams, there was no second chance.

When Dante finally woke up, some time past 4:00 a.m., he didn't bother trying to go back to sleep. He needed the rest, but it wouldn't be worth it if Serena came back to haunt him.

He watched Sara sleep, naked and satisfied in his bed. Her honey-blond hair was tousled. Yes, she was much less prim here, much less the mayor. There was so much more to her than the steadfast face she presented to the rest of the world. He saw it, even if no one else did. In that way she was entirely his. He knew her as no one else did.

Now and then she gathered flowers out of her garden, as well as a few blooms that grew wild, and arranged them in a haphazard way in hideously expensive and formal vases. In that way she marked these stuffy rooms as hers. He had caught her just yesterday, her fine hips swaying to the music from the radio as she plucked at long-stemmed wildflowers until they were arranged just so. He'd been so turned on at that moment he'd almost given in then and there. It was the hips that did it, not the flowers.

In her closet there were clothes he had never seen her wear. A red dress, a bohemian skirt and low-cut peasant blouse and a pair of incredibly high heels that screamed "take me, take me now" in particular caught his eye. The red dress still had the tag hanging from it, and the soles of the shoes had been unmarked. Still, she had bought them, which hinted at a woman very much unlike the prim and proper politician who was so intent on fulfilling her duties as a Vance and a Caldwell.

In Sara's collection of CDs there was a lot of classical music and jazz, but there was also Aretha Franklin and Prince and Bon Jovi and a collection of disco tunes created just for dancing. Disco. Who woulda thunk it?

He tried to imagine Sara wearing the red dress and the high heels, dancing to one of the CDs she'd shoved to the back of the storage case because they did not fit the image she had created for herself here. Unfortunately for him, he could imagine too well.

And again, unbidden, he thought of Serena. Sara roused thoughts and dreams of a woman lost because there was more here than just sex, just as there had been more with Serena. He didn't want more, and hadn't for a long time. *More* came with risk and pain. His life was filled with risk and pain of another sort, but he could handle physical challenges. It was the loss that had the ability to tear him up inside that he avoided these days.

It was almost five when Sara woke to find him staring at her. She smiled and reached out for him. "You're not sleeping."

"Neither are you," he countered, leaning down to kiss her throat. His hand slipped down her side to rest on one hip. He liked her curves, her womanly shape and warmth.

He didn't do anything more, since he'd already used the one condom he'd had stored in his wallet. Tonight, after he'd had a chance to stop by the drug store, he'd take care of her thoroughly—and not quite so quickly as he had last night.

But Sara didn't act as if she intended to stop. Her hands explored, more boldly than they had last night, until Dante had to move out of her reach. She wasn't insulted. She laughed and came after him, and soon she was straddling him.

He thought it best to stop her there and then. "I don't have another condom," he said. And he was quite sure she didn't have any sort of contraceptive in the house. Not Sara Vance, a woman who in the past few years had turned herself into the proper politician and grieving widow.

She didn't seem concerned. "I don't care."

"You should," he said.

She stared down at him, still and serious. "Are you sick?"

"No."

"It's the baby thing that worries you, I suppose," she said, sounding very unconcerned.

"Yes, it's the *baby thing*." How could she sound so calm?

She sighed. "I've actually been thinking about having a baby. I'm thirty-five, so it's almost too late. If I'm going to have children I need to get busy." A grin spread across her pretty face. "You would make a beautiful baby."

The statement was almost as effective as a bucket of ice water. "Naked and horny is really not the state to be in when you make such an important decision."

"I can't think of any better state to be in, can you?" she said, as she moved her body against his.

Not really, he conceded silently. It was a fine state. A blissful state....

He grabbed Sara and tossed her gently onto her back. She bounced and laughed, but when he spread her legs she stopped laughing. She was so beautiful, laid before him this way. She was a goddess, all curves and warmth and pleasure.

He took her mouth with his for a long, demanding kiss, and then he moved down to her throat. Her breasts. Her belly. His tongue tasted and explored. He kissed her until he could feel and taste her quiver. Every natural instinct within him told him to give her what she wanted. All of him; the possibility of life. But instead he reined in his primitive urges and with his tongue and fingers made her come so hard she rose up off the bed, her body jerking as she cried out softly.

Now that her physical needs had been met she would not think so fondly of taking a risk she had no business taking. Now she wouldn't ask too much of him.

"Wow." She breathed the word as her body collapsed. It seemed that she melted.

Dante left the bed quickly, and that's when Sara's eyes popped open. "Where are you going?" she asked sharply.

"I'm headed for a cold shower." The colder the better.

"Oh, no you don't," she said, scrambling from the bed.

He turned to face her, naked and fully aroused, more than a little annoyed, and wondering where the hell this was going. "Maybe you want babies, but I don't. It would be incredibly foolish for us to even think about unprotected sex, no matter how good the idea sounds at the moment. What part of *I'm not going to stay* didn't you understand?"

She looked a little hurt, but didn't give in to tears or accusations of her own. "Sorry," she said gently. "I didn't mean to pressure you, but I've just managed to let go of a past I was holding on to much too tightly, a past that was keeping me from living what's left of my life. I don't think it's a coincidence that it finally happened when you came back to town."

"I'm glad for you, I really am, but I haven't."

Her brow furrowed. "You haven't what?"

He hesitated for a moment before telling her the truth he denied to everyone else. Hell, he'd denied it to himself, too. "Let go of the past."

After that too-telling confession, he thought she'd let him shower in peace, but she didn't. Stubborn Sara followed him into the bathroom and into the shower. Silently she touched him, she kissed him, she stroked him, then she knelt down and put her mouth around him. With warm water raining down on them both, she made him come so hard he almost fell to his knees.

And then she stood and looked him in the eye. At the moment she was tenacious and brave, and very much the red-dress woman. "I won't ask more of you than you want to give," she said. "Not ever." Then she turned and left the shower with one last command. "Buy more condoms."

Chapter 6

Given the way the sock burning had gone last night, Sara expected Patty and/or Lydia to call and ask too many nosy questions. She certainly hadn't expected them to show up on her doorstep. Thank goodness Dante had run out to pick up a few things! She could only imagine the grilling he'd get from her sometimes overprotective friends if he was still there.

"Oh, my God, she did it," Patty said the moment she walked through the front door.

Lydia, slightly less enthusiastic, sighed. "Yeah, I can see."

Sara laughed as she closed the door behind her friends. "You can see what?"

"Your face," Patty said.

"That smile," Lydia added.

"And you laughed instead of telling us to mind our own business," Patty said.

"You're not wearing a bra," Lydia accused.

Again Sara laughed. "It's Sunday and I'm home alone. Why do I need a bra?"

"She's laughing again," Patty said, "and look at that glow! That glow could only come from really good sex. How was he? Studly? Impatient? *Very* patient? Traditional or kinky? Is he well endowed or is this glow and laughter the result of quality rather than quantity?"

Sara led the women into the parlor. "What if he's right around the corner listening?"

Patty snorted. "We waited until we saw his car pull away. Duh. We can't ask the questions we want to ask if he's here, now can we?"

"I imagine not," Sara conceded. "What if he hadn't left? How long were you willing to sit on the street and wait for him to leave?"

Lydia said, "We had a plan. I parked the car two doors down. If Dante hadn't left within an hour or so I was going to have Paul call and ask for some sort of manly help to get him out of the house. He said he'd loosen a board on the porch or knock down a section of fence, if necessary."

"Isn't that a bit extreme?" Sara asked.

"No!" her visitors said at the same time.

They all sat. "Dante won't be gone long," Sara said, "so let's get this over with."

"Do you love him?"

"If he hurts you, we'll break his legs."

"Is this *serious* or just a fling? He's definitely fling worthy."

"Okay, honestly, how good was it?"

"Quality or quantity?"

"You were careful, weren't you?"

The questions came, one right after the other, until Sara had to laugh. "I'm not answering these questions! I love both of you, and I appreciate your concern, but I'm allowed to keep a few things to myself." She held up a hand when they both started to argue. "I will tell you that I feel really good and really alive for the first time in a very long time. I won't say the word *love,* not yet, but I care about Dante and I think he cares about me. That's all you need to know." She looked at Patty, who had raised her finely sculpted dark eyebrows in friendly censure. "And who says a woman can't have both quality *and* quantity?"

Dante studied the display of personal items at the Tillman Pharmacy, which had opened at one o'clock on this quiet Sunday afternoon. The choices were surprisingly varied. Thin. Sensitive. Ribbed. Colored. Six-pack, twelve-pack, thirty-six pack.

He was about to just grab a twelve-pack when a tinny, shaky voice asked, "Need some help, young man?"

Dante turned his head to find an old woman who looked to be ninety if she was a day. She was stick-thin and wore her thin white hair in a bun. Thick black-rimmed glasses sat on a long nose, and she wore a white lab coat with the name of the pharmacy embroidered on the pocket. Great. She was trolling the condom section to scare off the customers.

"No thanks," he said. "I don't need any help."

"You don't want those," she said, snatching the twelve-pack from his hand and returning them to the shelf.

"I do, actually." He was not going back to Sara's house until he was well-prepared.

"I imagine a twelve-pack won't last a man like you a week. You look like a strapping, virile man to me, and goodness knows you don't want to run short. The price is much more reasonable per condom if you purchase the thirty-six pack, and there's a coupon inside. You can log onto the company's Web site and order the Novelties Variety Pack. With the coupon it's quite reasonable." She leaned in. "One hundred condoms and other assorted novelties."

"What sort of novelties?" Dante asked.

"I don't know but I'm dying to find out. Now, if you were to buy the thirty-six pack today and then order the variety pack online, you could drop by and let me know what that pack contains." She leaned in a bit closer and said, "I hear there are vibrating rings. I don't know what that might be, but it sounds intriguing, don't you think? There are also Triple Pleasure Dinger Rings. I looked them up on the Internet but the pictures I found were inadequate and my eyes aren't so good anymore."

Dante bought the thirty-six pack and left the pharmacy as quickly as possible, thankful that no one he knew had been shopping there at the same time. He had to be ten shades of crimson. Before he turned his car onto Sara's street he was laughing out loud.

Sara met him at the door and studied the large bag he held in one hand, raising her eyebrows slightly.

"Baby," he said, "you are mayor of one strange town."

He was taken by surprise when Patty and Lydia came walking out of the parlor before Sara had a chance to respond. The two women looked at him as if he'd sprouted a second head. They also studied the paper bag that had Tillman Pharmacy emblazed on one side. They smiled widely, and Patty bit her lip to keep from laughing. Lydia looked as much worried as amused.

He wondered for a moment what they'd been talking about before he'd arrived, but it didn't take him long to realize that he'd most likely been the subject of that conversation.

"We were just leaving," Lydia said, taking Patty's arm and leading her past Dante and Sara and toward the door. "Call us!" she cried as she opened the front door. "We'll do lunch!"

The door slammed, and they were alone. Sara took the bag from him and peeked inside. "I suppose this will do." She laughed lightly. "Think you got enough?"

Dante slipped his hand up her shirt to touch her bare breast. Right before he kissed her, he said, "For now."

Sara smiled as she pulled her Aretha Franklin CD out and put it in the stereo, which was discretely placed in the south parlor so it was handy but not prominent in the old-fashioned room. Dante wasn't home yet, and Opal had just left for the day.

Since coming back to Tillman she'd spent many, many hours alone in this house, but in the past it had always felt as if she'd been trapped in a prison. A pretty, well-furnished, elegant prison but, still, a prison. She had never lived here with Robert and she had not grown up in this house, as he had. It had been a place to come after her life had fallen apart. It was an obligation, the same way her new job was an obligation.

Dante had been living there for a matter of days, and suddenly this house she had mentally compared to a mausoleum on more than one occasion didn't feel like an obligation. It felt like a home. There was love and laughter in the air. There was passion and life here, in a way there had never been before.

Sara kicked off her shoes and slipped off her moss-green jacket, and she began to dance. "Respect" was playing, so how could she not dance? After a few bars she began to sing. She would never sing in public—that was her gift to the public—but when she was alone she could lose herself in the music and the song. Even when "Respect" was done, she continued to dance and sing—when she could remember the words. She didn't listen to this CD often enough. There wasn't always enough room in the parlor for the dance moves that seemed appropriate, so now and then she slipped into the foyer to dance.

The phone rang while she was in the foyer, and she rushed into the parlor to turn down the stereo before she reached for the receiver.

"Hello?" she said breathlessly, wondering if it was Dante calling to tell her he'd be late, or asking about supper or just checking in.

For a moment no one responded, but then she heard someone breathe. If it was a wrong number, why didn't they just apologize and hang up? She was about to return the receiver to the cradle when the caller whispered, "You're making a terrible mistake."

Sara realized she had made many terrible mistakes but had no idea which one this caller was speaking of.

She had caller ID on some of the phones in the house but not on this one. "Who is this?"

There was no answer to that question. She could check the caller ID log on one of the other phones when she was finished here, but that didn't do her any good at the moment. Was this call about Tillman business or one of her charities or was it related to her recent personal troubles? Her heart hitched. As the silence continued, she became more and more certain that this call had nothing to do with her work in the mayor's office.

"Get rid of him," the caller whispered.

"Get rid of who?" she asked, knowing very well who the caller spoke of but hoping that if they talked long enough he—or she—would say enough to reveal his identity. A word, a turn of phrase...something.

"You know damn well who I'm talking about!" There was anger in the husky whisper, but Sara still couldn't tell if the caller was a man or a woman.

"There are a number of city employees..."

"Mangino," the whisperer said. "He has no business in that house. He has no business in Tillman. If you know what's good for you, you'll send him away."

She'd been so focused on the caller she hadn't heard Dante's car pull into the driveway, but she couldn't miss the opening of the front door and the clicking sound of his fingers against the security alarm keyboard. She moved to the parlor doorway and waved him over, covering the mouthpiece with her hand. "I think it's him," she whispered.

Dante took the phone and listened for a moment, then he said, "Hello?"

His eyes caught and held hers, and then he pulled the phone away from his ear. "He hung up. What did he say?"

"He or she," Sara said. "I couldn't be sure." She then told him what the caller had said, and they walked to the kitchen to check the caller ID there. The call had come up as private, and Dante rolled his eyes in disgust. "You can fix it so no private calls come through, you know."

"It hasn't been a problem before this," she said calmly.

His jaw hardened in that way it did when he got tense or worried. "It's a problem now. Someone doesn't want me here."

Sara wrapped her arms around his neck. "Of course the coward who stole my underwear and then replaced it doesn't want you here. No one's going to dare to bother me while you're in the house."

"I won't be here forever," he said.

"I know." She smiled at him, in spite of the pain his words brought her. "But you're here now." And as hard as it was to believe, that was enough. Sara was scared of losing her heart to Dante. She was taking a chance, not with her safety but with the part of her soul she'd buried for so long. For the first time in her life, Sara was perfectly content to live in the moment, and for a woman who was terrified of losing again, that was a miracle.

Dante grinned at the older woman who served him a big, hot breakfast. Opal seemed to be warming up to him, slowly but surely, which made living at Sara's house easier than it had been for the first few days. He was beginning to get very comfortable here. The fact that they'd been moving back and forth between his bedroom and hers for the past five days didn't hurt matters at all.

He only occasionally got antsy because he was starting to feel at home here. Settling down wasn't in his plans and never had been. He had a small house in the country not much more than three hours from Tillman and not too far from Bennings' headquarters, but he was rarely there for more than a week at a time. As for family, he and his mother were not what he'd call close. He made short visits to her condo in Orlando, a small and very Florida-flavored home she shared with her third husband, Richard, but he never stayed for more than two days. She hassled him about his hair and tattoos and told him, if he didn't get married soon, she'd never live to see her grandchildren, and he called her husband Dickie. He hadn't been down that way in about four years and had no desire to visit anytime soon.

She hadn't been all that great at the single-mother thing, not then and not now. He supposed some women had the maternal gene and some didn't. His mother had been angry with her husband for dying so soon and leaving her with a child to raise on her own. She had never missed an opportunity to mention that Dante was a difficult child, too much like his father.

She had blamed the failure of her second marriage on her only child. Sure, she'd been hurting at the time, but he'd been eight years old, and he'd hurt, too.

Sara hadn't mentioned motherhood again, thank God. Dante didn't plan to get married and coach Little League, and he wouldn't leave a child in the position he'd grown up in. True, his father had died, not run out on them because he didn't want a family, but the end result would be the same.

Even though he knew Sara would do a much better job than his mother had.

"You know, my son is about your age," Opal said as she refilled his coffee. "I can't get him to settle down, either." She smiled. "There was a time when boys your age would've been married for a good fifteen years or more and become fathers by now. What are you waiting for?"

Did Opal think he'd marry Sara and settle in here for good? Even though it might make his stay easier if the protective housekeeper believed that his intentions were honorable, as they said, he wouldn't lead her, or Sara, on. "What's your son's excuse?" He was sure this was a frequent subject of conversation.

Opal sighed. "Elliott says he's waiting for the right girl to come along. Is that your excuse?"

"Nope," he said as he grabbed a piece of bacon from his plate. "I don't think there is such a thing as the right girl. Not for me."

She scoffed a bit but didn't seem inclined to argue.

Sara came into the room and everything changed. She smiled at him and the room seemed brighter; the air smelled fresher. His skin tingled. Dangerous stuff.

"You look very mayoral," he said, taking in her plain dark blue suit and sensible heels. Even her hair was restrained this morning, caught up in a sedate bun.

Even though this was the life she had embraced, this prim woman before him was not the true Sara. He knew it, even if no one else did. He'd seen the red dress hanging in her closet; he'd caught her dancing when she thought no one was watching. She was a woman who gave all of herself without fear, without asking for more than he had to give.

"I have a meeting with the city council this afternoon," she said, wrinkling her nose. "What about you?"

"More training for the new recruits. Marksmanship." Training was much preferable to the investigations he'd been involved in so far. He'd been looking into petty thefts and pranks, for the most part, though there had been a drug bust on Monday. Exciting stuff. Sam Terrell had been in possession of prescription medicines that were not his own. Sam Terrell was eighty-seven.

He'd been promised some sort of report on the underwear he'd sent to Bennings more than a week ago. They were significantly faster than the state lab, though they'd had to bump his request back for a few days to make time for a "real" case and a paying client.

He couldn't deny that he and Sara were getting closer—maybe too close—but she did know where to draw the line. She hadn't asked him about the past he'd said he couldn't forget, not one time, and she didn't ask him how long he was going to stay. She took one day at a time without pressure, without demands, without questions.

Opal glanced from him to Sara and back again, her eyes calculating. She had to know they were lovers. In addition to her other duties, the woman sometimes made the beds. Since she'd come back to work on Monday, she had to notice that only one bed or the other had been slept in, never both.

And here she was grilling him about marriage. A basic instinct screamed at Dante to leave. Jesse had managed to sign on a couple of new recruits, and while they were as green as hell, they were capable enough. The dreams of Serena had not stopped. In fact, they'd grown more frequent and more intense. She'd started talking to him—which was preferable to watching her die again and again but was still disturbing.

Last night Serena had asked him why he didn't write limericks anymore. In truth, she had been horrified by his lowly and often crude idea of poetry, but she had also laughed at his efforts. She had laughed and grabbed him and ripped off his clothes....

If not for the one anonymous phone call Sara had gotten, Dante might convince himself that there was no danger here and he was free to go. That one seemingly harmless call bothered him. Someone wanted him gone. That likely meant they had plans for Sara after his departure. How could he leave?

How could he stay?

He was sitting at the kitchen table, thinking about leaving Tillman tonight or tomorrow, considering making other arrangements for Sara's safety and getting out while the getting was good, when his cell phone rang. A quick check of the caller ID showed it was Jesse calling from his own cell phone. Dante answered, expecting an invitation to Little League practice, or maybe a change in the training schedule.

He knew that was wrong the moment he heard Jesse's tense voice. He realized how wrong when Jesse said, "I need you pronto. We have a murder."

Dante got the basic facts from Jesse via cell phone while he drove to the crime scene, a small house on the edge of town. The young woman, the victim, had been found by her husband, who worked the night shift at the textile factory, which employed so many Tillman residents.

His suspicions went immediately to the husband, who had called in the murder. Domestic violence, jealousy, an argument that got out of hand... How many times had he seen a man cry over a woman when he'd damn near killed her with his rage? How many times had he seen a man declare love for a woman while he made her life hell? *Love* was just another word for *passion,* and passion was one step away from rage.

Ain't love grand?

The house was on the north edge of town, situated on a large grassy lot that was only minimally cared for. A portion of the yard had been mowed, but those who lived there had apparently never heard of a weed eater. Dante looked for signs that children might live there, but saw no toys in the yard or on the front porch. There was no swing set, at least not one that was visible. From the driveway he could see a large portion of the back-yard, where there was a dormant garden area and a clothesline. A white blouse and a man's blue shirt whipped in the breeze.

Neither the coroner nor the paramedics had arrived, although Dante assumed they, as well as uniformed of-ficers to contain the scene, were right behind him. The husband was sitting on the front steps with Jesse, wait-ing for help to arrive. Red-eyed and shaking, the man sitting there looked whipped and stunned. Dante saw no evidence of anger in the young man, who was probably no older than twenty-five.

As Dante walked toward the front porch, Jesse made

quick introductions. "Sergeant Mangino, this is Henry Phillips. He found his wife's body when he came home from working the night shift at the factory."

A bleary-eyed Henry looked to Dante and nodded. "Maddie's usually waiting for me and we have break-fast together. She didn't like me working night shift, but she always woke up early and made me breakfast, and we talked about work before I went to bed." His eyes looked distant for a moment, but he forced himself to snap out of it. "Chief, after I talked to you I didn't touch anything else in the house, I swear. I kinda wanted to stay inside and keep Maddie company until someone got here to take care of her, but I couldn't stay in there and look at her anymore," Henry said. "She doesn't even look like herself, but I know it's her. I can tell that much. Who would do something like this?" He grabbed Jesse's shirt in one small fist. "Who?"

Jesse very gently removed Henry's hand from his shirt. "Dante, let's step inside." The chief provided gloves for both of them. In the near distance, sirens wailed.

Henry stepped back, making way for the two law en-forcement officers to step into the house and study the scene of his wife's murder. Jesse moved forward, but Dante hesitated. There was a dead woman in that house. Was her throat cut, as Serena's had been cut? Was there blood everywhere, or had someone choked the life out of her without spilling a drop?

In the years since Serena's death Dante had buried himself in work, but he was always involved before violence occurred. He worked as a bodyguard or as a private investigator. If police presence became neces-sary, his job was done and he walked away. Until now.

He followed in Jesse's footsteps, and behind them Henry started to cry. If he'd killed her, he was a damn good actor, and Dante didn't think that was the case. So, who had done it? Had Maddie been screwing around on her adoring husband? Had she been seeing a man prone to violence while her husband worked the night shift? Did she owe someone money? Were there drugs involved?

Dante took a deep, stilling breath before following Jesse into the small house.

The dimly lit living room was just inside the front door. One end-table lamp burned. The television was on, but the sound had been muted. Maddie Phillips's body was sprawled on the living-room floor, fully dressed and very dead. Her throat had not been cut, but there was blood, and plenty of it. She'd been stabbed at least four times with a kitchen knife, which was lying on the carpet beside her. For a moment Dante's head swam and he had a spell of tunnel vision, but he pulled himself back and gritted his teeth. Dammit, Maddie was no older than her husband. She didn't even look to be twenty-two.

"Okay," Jesse said in a soft voice, his eyes on the dead girl. "Look around. Tell me what you see."

Dante longed for boring duties like grilling pretty mayors about stolen underwear, or talking to hysterical old ladies about broken windows and wayward base-balls, as he used his years of experience to study the crime scene. No, this was not his normal job, but he had learned to be observant, and very little rattled him.

This rattled.

"Door's not busted, so if the killer came in through the front, she let him in. All the doors and windows

should be checked just in case, but look at her." He
gestured with a hand. "She's not much more than a
child, and children are trusting. They never think anything bad will happen to them." When you're young
and in love, there's always tomorrow. You're invul-
nerable. "The only visible wounds are the stab
wounds, so I'd say the killer took her by surprise and
by the time she thought to fight back, it was too late.
She's got long fingernails and they're all intact, but
you will want them checked for possible skin and
DNA. Maybe she got a scratch in before she died." He
hoped so.

"We'll have to interrogate the husband," Jesse said.

"Yeah, but he didn't do it."

"I know."

"Find out if she was using any kind of drugs, if he
suspected her of cheating, if they owed anyone a lot of
money…" Dante made himself look at Maddie once
again, and this time something caught his eye. An
emerald-green bra strap barely peeked out of her blood-
stained blue T-shirt. His heart damn near stopped. What
were the odds?

Dante turned on his heel and returned to the porch,
where Henry once again sat on the steps, numb and pale
and shaking.

"Henry, have y'all had anything come up missing
lately?"

The kid didn't rise from the step, but turned his head
and looked up. "Missing?"

Dante didn't want to feed the kid any more than was
necessary, but he had to know and he had to know *now*.
"Stolen. Have you had any thefts here?"

"No," Henry said. "This is a safe neighborhood. Do you think I'd leave Maddie alone at night in a house that wasn't safe?"

Dante breathed a sigh of relief. There were probably millions of green bras just that color floating around out there. He was about to return to the house and its horrors when Henry said, "Well, a couple weeks ago we did have some clothes come up missing off the line, but I think that was those teenagers from down the street, the ones that whistle at Maddie when they drive by and we're sitting out on the porch. Whoever it was felt guilty, I guess, because a few days later they left some new, uh, personal items, on the porch. They were trying to make things right, I guess."

The bottom dropped out of Dante's stomach. "Describe these personal items."

Henry stood, and Dante became aware that Jesse was standing in the doorway, right behind him. "What the hell is this?" the kid shouted. "My wife is *dead,* and you're standing here asking me about some old clothes that were stolen off the line? You're asking me about the stuff that was left on the porch? What's wrong with you? Get in there and find some evidence to get the son of a bitch who did this! Stop wasting my time and yours!"

Dante remained calm. "I don't think I'm wasting anyone's time."

A police car and an ambulance pulled sharply into the yard.

Henry went very still. "You think the same SOB…" His face paled and he swayed.

"I can't know that, but we have to follow every lead, don't we?"

Henry nodded. "What was taken off the line was old underwear, not even worth reporting stolen. The things that were brought by here a few days later looked to be a lot more expensive. There was a red-and-black bra and panties, and a set of dark green underthings. Maddie liked them," he said softly. "She thought they were pretty and feminine."

The paramedics ran for the porch, and although they bustled, Dante knew they were much too late. A coroner and a crime-lab team were all that was needed here.

Dante looked at his cousin. Everything that needed to be done here could wait. "I've gotta run."

Sara was sitting at her desk planning the afternoon meeting, thinking of going home early even though there was a pile of correspondence in front of her that she had no hope of finishing before her meeting with the city council, and she had three phone calls to return. Phone calls she didn't want to make. It was going to be a long day. She hadn't slept well last night, hadn't slept much at all since Saturday night, so maybe an early day was called for.

When her grandfather had passed away after serving five terms as mayor of Tillman, several of his friends and cronies had turned to her and asked that she run for the office. The family connections—Caldwell and Vance—would get her in, they assured her. She hadn't been so sure. It was her duty, they said, to carry on the family tradition. She'd still hesitated. When they'd argued that it was what her grandfather would have wanted, she'd given in. They had all known she'd do anything for her Papa, whether he remained among the living or not.

There was a cursory knock on her door, and then it opened swiftly. Somehow she was not surprised to see Dante walk in, even though it hadn't been that long since he'd taken off at a run to meet Jesse at a murder scene. Murder in Tillman. That seemed so wrong.

Dante's eyes were narrowed, and his entire body was tense. He actually conducted a quick sweep of the room with those calculating eyes, as if looking for someone else. Why was he here so soon? She would have thought that perhaps the reported murder had been false, but it was clear by his body language that all was not well.

"What's happened?" she asked.

He closed the door behind him and then walked toward her, stopping on the other side of the desk to lean in and glare at her. "I screwed up, big-time."

"How?"

"I sent your anonymous underwear to Bennings last week, which means they were out of official custody. If any fingerprints are found, they won't hold up in court."

Why was he talking about that problem now? "I thought we decided legalities weren't a factor."

He hesitated, and she could almost see the wheels turning in his head, as he searched for a way to respond. That was when she knew this was *very* bad.

"There was another incident. I believe the same man stole another woman's things off the line and replaced them with garments identical to the ones which were left for you. Just as in your case, a box was dropped on the front porch."

She wanted to think that they had a serial underwear bandit on their hands, but knowing that Dante had left her house that morning to go to a murder scene, and judging the seriousness of his demeanor, she knew it was much worse than that.

He confirmed it. "Sometime early this morning or late last night, Maddie Phillips was murdered. We can't be sure, not yet, but your underwear thief is suspect number one in my mind."

Sara's stomach dropped out from under her, making her glad she'd remained seated. "Maddie Phillips," she said.

"Yes. Did you know her?" He seemed very interested, and she knew he was searching for links, for clues. For suspects.

"I went to school with her aunt, and her husband works at my cousin Owen's textile factory." Again, her stomach flipped. "Oh, poor Henry. He adored Maddie. They were high school sweethearts." Her eyes filled with tears. She knew what it was like to lose a loved one. Even with illness and time to say goodbye, it was hard. Horribly hard. To lose someone you loved in such a violent and sudden way was unthinkable.

"You're going to be under twenty-four-hour guard," Dante said sharply.

"We can't even be sure…"

"Until we are sure it's the underwear perv who killed Maddie Phillips, or not, you're under twenty-four-hour guard," Dante interrupted tersely. "At work, at home, getting from one place to another, at sock burnings… you will not be alone. You don't go to the bathroom without an escort."

"That seems a bit extreme. Is it really necessary? I do understand that caution is called for, but…"

The Reader Service — Here's how it works:

BUSINESS REPLY MAIL

FIRST-CLASS MAIL   PERMIT NO. 717   BUFFALO, NY

POSTAGE WILL BE PAID BY ADDRESSEE

SILHOUETTE READER SERVICE
3010 WALDEN AVE
PO BOX 1867
BUFFALO NY 14240-9952

NO POSTAGE
NECESSARY
IF MAILED
IN THE
UNITED STATES

Dante put his hands on her desk and leaned in. "I think Maddie Phillips let her killer into the house, which means she likely knew him. She was stabbed a minimum of four times with a kitchen knife that had a blade which looked to be five-and-a-half inches long and two inches wide at the base. She didn't even have a chance to put up a fight, it happened so fast."

Sara swallowed hard. The picture Dante painted was more than clear enough. "Fine. If you think it's best."

"I do."

"I'm sure Chief Edwards can come up with a few officers who can…"

"I'll handle it," Dante said.

"Don't you think the chief should handle the assignments?" she asked, grateful for his concern but at the same time annoyed that he was taking over. Yes, they were sleeping together, but he'd made it very clear that they didn't have anything else. He wasn't going to stay. His presence in her life was wonderful but temporary. There was no reason for him to be so possessive.

Dammit, he couldn't have it both ways—he couldn't insist that they keep an emotional distance and at the same time behave like a caveman protecting his territory.

"No," he said sharply. "Jesse worked homicide in Birmingham for a few years, so he'll know how to handle the murder investigation. Surveillance and bodyguard duty are my specialty, not his. Hell, it's not as if Tillman can afford the extra man hours." His lips thinned. "And it's not as if I can trust these yokels."

"So, you're going to watch me twenty-four hours a day, now?"

"Nope. Only eight. Two more Bennings agents are already on their way. We'll each take an eight-hour shift."

The man standing before her was intense and dedicated. Although she didn't want him to know it, deep down she was relieved that he was taking charge. Although she did her best not to show it, she was scared out of her wits.

"I suppose that will work, but it's really very presumptuous of you to make arrangements without speaking to me first. What if I hadn't agreed to your suggestion?"

Dante glared at her with eyes such a dark brown they were almost black. She had come to love those eyes all over again, even when they were hard, as they were now. "What makes you think it was ever a suggestion?"

Chapter 7

The Phillips house was cordoned off with yellow tape, and Maddie Phillips's body had been taken away. Dante stood on the front porch with Jesse, who was none too happy with him for sending the underwear that had been left on Sara's porch to Bennings for analysis, and not entirely pleased that he'd called in two other agents for mayoral guard duty even though he grudgingly admitted the city didn't have the manpower for the job.

Since they thus far had found no significant evidence at the murder scene, odds were they wouldn't find prints on the box or the underwear. A panty thief might be careless. A killer, less so. Dante wished there were techs in the house finding identifiable fibers and minuscule hairs, but this wasn't television and it wasn't so easy.

The house was surrounded by television crews, as well as photographers and journalists from a number of

North Alabama newspapers. The grisly murder of a young woman was news. The reporters all stayed beyond the yellow tape and watched, occasionally making a note or taking a picture.

Jesse waved Dante to his side, and when he was there by the porch railing Jesse pointed to a spot on the ground and said softly, "Our picture's going to be in the newspaper tomorrow." Sure enough, every camera in the vicinity turned to them. Some were silent. Others clicked and whirred. "I'm not sure what it is about pointing," Jesse said, "but they love it."

Dante was less than amused, and his cousin saw his displeasure.

A wrinkle—was it new?—deepened between bushy blond eyebrows. "Yes, dammit, I know a young woman is dead. It's tragic. It's heartbreaking. But I swear, Dante, in my career I've worked too many murders not to learn when to let loose, even if just for a minute or two," Jesse said as he dropped his hand. "Sometimes you have to laugh or scream or cry just to survive, just to stay sane while insane things are going on around you."

"I want this bastard," Dante said.

"So do I."

"But for me, Sara is top priority," Dante clarified. He remembered his first sight of Maddie Phillips and felt his stomach turn over. "I won't lose another one."

Jesse nodded.

After Serena had been killed, Dante hadn't been able to tell just anyone what had happened, but he'd told Jesse. He'd liked the math teacher a lot, even though she'd been older, smarter, and not at all his type. If she hadn't been killed, maybe whatever they'd had would've run its course and ended naturally in a few weeks or a few months, but he'd never know. She'd been murdered just to send him and the other agents at the all-girls school a message. *I'm here. I know who you are. Watch your step.* She'd been killed because he'd made the mistake of getting involved with her. He'd screwed up and she'd paid with her life.

He had never been able to forgive himself for not being there when she'd needed him.

Jesse sighed in what seemed to be pure disgust. "I'm glad you and Sara hooked up again, I really am, but dammit, this isn't the way things were supposed to work out."

Dante hadn't told his cousin that he and Sara were sleeping together, but it seemed that everyone in town knew they were involved. His car was parked outside her house every night, and if the old lady in the pharmacy was a gossip, all guesswork had been taken out of the equation. Dante didn't care what anyone thought, and apparently neither did Sara.

"This turn of events was nowhere in the plan." Jesse sounded decidedly guilty.

Suddenly suspicious, Dante glared at his cousin. "What plan?"

Yep, Jesse looked *very* guilty. "Okay, here goes. A couple of months ago I got a phone call from your boss, Cal."

Dante still had a hard time thinking of Quinn Calhoun as "boss" but that was right enough, these days. Already, he didn't like the sound of this conversation. "A phone call about what?" As if he didn't know.

"You," Jesse said sharply. "Cal was worried. They all were. You weren't getting over the girl, even though it's been just short of six years. No one's saying it wasn't a tragedy, but what happened wasn't your fault and there was nothing to be done. Cal said you were still throwing yourself into your work a bit too much, volunteering for the most dangerous jobs, getting more and more reclusive as the years went past instead of actually getting better. We all thought maybe you should get away for a while. Sometimes a change of scenery is a good thing."

Dante wondered how the press would react if he tackled the chief. Talk about getting their picture in the paper... "So, my stay in Tillman was supposed to be, what, a vacation?"

"Yeah, more or less. Life in Tillman is usually very low key. We figured you could spend time with the kids, toss the football around, have Sunday dinner with the family, investigate a few minor crimes, maybe spend some time with an old girlfriend...."

"And yet here we are," Dante said sharply. "Someone's been harassing Sara, and a young woman is dead. Not exactly low key in my book."

"Yeah, I know."

"Hell, Jesse. I cut my hair for this freakin' job."

Jesse managed a small smile. "I did expect more of a fight out of you on that point. Still, it is city policy, and you didn't put up much of an argument."

"It's hair. It'll grow back." Dante didn't want to admit as much, but when Jesse had asked him for this favor, he'd realized it was time for him to step back, to re-assess, to make a few changes in his life. Not that being a small-town cop was on the agenda for the years to come, but spending a few months in Tillman hadn't seemed like a bad idea when Jesse had first mentioned the idea. Even if it had meant cutting off the hair he'd worn long for most of his adult life. He'd cut it for the Marines, years ago, and he hadn't seen this as being much different. Rebelling at seventeen and refusing to cut his hair was one thing; digging in over something so trivial at thirty-five was just sad. He didn't want to be one of those old guys with a thin gray ponytail and a pissy attitude.

Didn't this change everything? He wasn't helping out his cousin; Jesse was trying to help him. Cal, too. Dante didn't know if he should be angry or thankful. They were wrong to interfere in his life, but it wasn't as if they didn't have a point.

Still, he knew what he had to do. "I quit."

"You can't quit!" Jesse responded. "Maybe I did get you here on a bit of a false pretense, but I do need the manpower. That part of it wasn't a lie."

"You need cops," Dante said. "I'm not a cop."

"So you're going to quit."

"Yep. You've got a few new hires to take up the slack. You'll be fine."

"You're going to up and leave Tillman right in the middle of a crisis," Jesse said, his anger building. "Right when I need you the most, you're going to cut out on me."

"Nope," Dante said, "I'm not leaving."

There was that brow wrinkle again. "You just said…"

"I said I was quitting." Dante loosened his tie. He was already damned tired of wearing the brightly colored nooses, and would not mind leaving them behind. "I didn't say I was leaving Tillman."

"You're sticking around on your own time," Jesse said.

"Yeah." Until he knew Sara was safe, he couldn't walk away. Dante leaned over the porch railing and pointed at a bare spot on the ground. Jesse automatically followed his direction and looked to the ground as Dante said, "Smile. Your picture's going to be in the paper tomorrow."

Her meeting with the city council had been cancelled, and she'd gotten the early day she'd been thinking of this morning—but not at all in the way she'd planned. Sara sat in the south parlor, a book she could not read clutched in her hands, a classical CD that should've been soothing playing softly in the background. She barely heard the music, and the book was nothing but a prop to keep the strange men in her house from trying to make idle conversation.

What she'd been so sure was a minor crime committed by a pervert was very possibly the act of a killer. Someone she knew, perhaps. Someone who had been in her backyard and on her front porch and beneath her bedroom window. Someone who had killed Maddie Phillips.

The two men Dante had left her with were quiet and efficient, alert and unobtrusive. They rarely spoke, and since she'd claimed a chair in the parlor and picked up an unfinished book, they hadn't said a word to her. Now and then they would make a sweep of her large house, walking through every room, checking all the doors and windows. The blond one was called Hawkins and the other, the older man with no hair at all, responded to Potts. They were polite and efficient, and she felt much safer with them in the house. She was quite sure these two men would throw themselves between her and a bullet without hesitation. Shielding her was their job, their calling.

And yet she wanted Dante with her now. He could be annoying as all get out when it suited him, but when he was with her, she felt safer.

When the doorbell rang, Sara nearly jumped out of her skin. Hawkins made his way to the door, cautious, armed, but not outwardly alarmed.

Sara looked up at Potts. "Dante wouldn't ring the doorbell."

The gruff man responded. "If he doesn't want to get shot, he would." Judging by his manner it was supposed to be a joke. She didn't think it was at all funny.

"It's Mangino," Hawkins called from the foyer.

The relief that rushed through Sara was too strong to ignore.

Dante walked into the parlor, looking very different than he had when she'd seen him last. He was in blue jeans and a plain gray T-shirt that allowed her to see the now-familiar tattoo on his forearm. It was a dragon surrounded by curling designs that looked rather Celtic in nature. All his tattoos were stark and crisp, without the softness of color. They marked his life as hard, unyielding.

Sara did not even have a small butterfly tattoo or a gentle dolphin. She'd always been afraid of the pain—and even more afraid that after the tattooing was done, she'd change her mind.

Dante headed straight for her. "Any news?" she asked.

"Only that I quit my job."

Her heart leaped more than a little. "You quit? Why?" She tried not to sound devastated.

"I'm not a cop."

She sounded a little testy when she asked, "Well, what are you, then?" She could already imagine him leaving. She could see him walking out her front door without looking back. Oh, he'd make sure Hawkins and Potts or others like them were around to protect her for as long as was necessary, but that didn't mean he'd stay.

The expression on his face was one of restrained amusement. Those eyebrows lifted slightly. The lips curled, but just a little. "I'm the guy who gets things done, sweetheart. I'm the man who does the jobs no one else wants."

"Like cleaning toilets and digging ditches?"

"Like finding people who don't want to be found, and keeping stubborn, pretty mayors alive."

She couldn't argue with that one.

Potts approached, and Dante turned to face him.

The bald man nodded his big head. "Man, you sure do look different without the hair."

Without the hair? Dante had a thick head of hair, one any woman would kill for.

"It'll grow back," Dante said. "Y'all can head for the hotel and get some rest. I'm in for the night."

Sara tried not to let her relief show. No longer a Tillman employee or not, he wasn't leaving her. Not tonight, anyway.

"I'm taking the 7:00 a.m. to 3:00 p.m. shift," Potts said, "so I'll see you here in the morning. Hawkins will take three to eleven, and like you said earlier, you get the graveyard shift."

"Just meet us at the courthouse in the morning." Dante looked down at her, once again all business in his attitude. "Eightish?"

"I try to be there no later than seven-fifty."

Again he smiled, before returning his attention to Potts. "You heard the woman. No later than seven-fifty."

Potts nodded, then he collected Hawkins. The two men left by way of the front door, and Sara heard Dante lock the door behind them. A lock clicked softly, a bolt slid home. And then she heard his footsteps on the hardwood floor, solid, steady steps that came slowly and surely closer.

When Dante stepped into the parlor, Sara was very aware that they were once again alone.

"I wish you hadn't quit." Since he was no longer employed there, he could leave at any time. He'd made it very clear that he wasn't going to stay, but now the time of his departure seemed so much closer. "What happens now?"

Dante leaned against the doorjamb, more casual than she'd seen him since he'd gotten that phone call that morning, and yet just as coiled and tense. "You go about your usual routine, and we stay close."

Close and armed, judging by what she'd seen thus far. "For how long?"

"Until we know for sure that someone besides the underwear thief killed Maddie Phillips, or we catch him."

"That could be a long time."

"Yes, it could."

His eyes caught and held hers. He looked different,

now that he had this new duty. This was the man he had become after leaving her all those years ago. She'd realized from the start that he was a hard man. At this moment she finally realized how hard.

Opal had left a couple of hours ago, and now Dante's coworkers were gone. She'd spent many hours alone with Dante in the past few days, so she didn't hesitate to put her book aside and walk to him, easing herself into his arms, resting her head against his chest.

"I'm glad you're here," she said softly.

His arms wrapped easily around her. "Me, too. Don't worry. I won't let anyone hurt you."

She believed him.

It was amazing how easily she had taken to being his lover. She was a traditional girl and it was foolish to get involved with a man who continued to declare that he would not stay any longer than was necessary, and still—being with Dante felt very right.

She kissed him, deeply and with a passion she had once thought was long gone from her life and her body. Instantly they were connected, and whatever horrors the day had brought were dismissed—at least for a while. She broke the kiss just long enough to say, "Opal left a casserole in the fridge. Are you hungry?"

Dante lifted her off her feet. "No. You?"

She shook her head as she wrapped her legs around his hips. Her skirt rode up on her thighs.

"Pantyhose," Dante said with disdain as he carried her toward the stairs. "Hate 'em."

"Me, too," she said honestly.

"I like you bare-legged and braless," he said.

In spite of the seriousness of the day, she managed

a smile. "I doubt that dress code would go over well at city hall."

"Then don't go to city hall," he said as they reached the top of the stairs. "Work from home. It'll be easier for me to keep an eye on you that way."

"I can hardly spend all day here with you, bare-legged and braless."

He drew back the covers on her bed and then dropped her. She landed with a gentle bounce, and before she'd stopped bouncing he was taking off her shoes. "Why not?" he asked.

He didn't expect an answer, and she didn't offer one.

Dante pushed her skirt high with his big, warm hands, and snagged the waistband of her pantyhose and panties. He drew them down and off, moving almost impatiently. Since their first night together, he had not shown even a hint of impatience in the bedroom, but now he moved as if he could not bare her body quickly enough. He dropped the garments he'd removed to the floor, and then ran his hands up her bare thighs, pushing her skirt higher, teasing her with his fingertips, leaning over her to take a long, deep kiss.

He managed to unbutton her blouse and unsnap her bra, and just enough fabric was pushed aside to free one breast, which he kissed with fervor. When he drew her nipple into his mouth, she almost came up off the bed. Her thighs wrapped around him, her body instinctively pulled closer to his.

She reached between their bodies to unzip his jeans and push them lower, and she took him in her hand. How could she want him so much, how could she need him so badly she was able to forget everything else?

There was a short delay, when Dante reached into her bedside drawer for a condom and quickly sheathed himself in it. No matter how carried away he seemed to be, he never forgot to be careful. She supposed she should be grateful one of them could think as they got closer and closer to coming together.

With clothes askew and more on than off, Dante filled her aching body. She could almost cry with the relief, with the pleasure that began as soon as he was inside her. Like their first time, this was fast and furious and frantic, as if they were still young and innocent, as if they might never have this opportunity again. Her orgasm came too soon and unbelievably hard, as she ground her hips against Dante's and gave a soft, instinctive cry. He pumped harder and faster, and then he gave over to physical release, to pleasure and more than pleasure.

Tears filled her eyes. She couldn't help them, didn't fight the sting. She didn't sob, but the emotion that rushed through her was impossible to ignore. If she thought he'd stay, she might cry and laugh at the same time, but she knew this love affair was temporary. No matter how much it would hurt when he left, she wasn't sorry. She felt alive again, nowhere more than in this bed, in his arms.

He didn't immediately leave her, but gave her a long, slow kiss. "I thought about you all day."

Knowing him, that meant he'd worried all day. "Lately I've been thinking about you an awful lot myself," she confessed. She felt as if they had much more than just sex, but she was afraid to push, afraid to ask for more from a man who had made it clear he didn't have more to offer.

Dante pushed a strand of hair out of her face. "We need to talk," he said.

Her heart constricted. He sounded much too serious. "I don't want to talk, not tonight."

"Neither do I, but it's time." He kissed her again. "I'm going to put the casserole in the oven. When you're ready, come on downstairs. This is a kitchen conversation."

"I like pillow talk much better," she whispered. Kitchen conversation sounded ominous.

Dante smiled, which did remove some of her fears. "So do I, but this needs to be said."

More rules, she imagined. More declarations of what they could not have, when she was so very happy with what they did have. "Fine," she conceded. "You put the casserole in while I take a quick shower."

He straightened his clothes and headed for the hallway bathroom, somewhat lost in thought—no doubt preparing himself for their kitchen conversation.

When Dante was gone she sat up and listened as he moved around down the hallway. Maybe things were not as bad as she thought they might be. Surely he wouldn't make love to her and then tell her he was done. Temporary or not, it was too soon to lose what they'd found—much too soon. Surely he wouldn't get carried away physically and then almost immediately turn around and tell her this wasn't working out the way he'd planned.

Surely he wouldn't. So why was her heart beating so hard she could feel it pounding in her chest? She hadn't had Dante back in her life nearly long enough to deal with losing him all over again.

* * *

Dante was comfortable in the kitchen of this big old house. He'd learned to cook years ago—not that there was much skill required in sticking a prepared casserole in the oven.

Outwardly he remained calm, but inside he was spinning. Coming to Tillman was meant to be temporary. He'd thought he was doing Jesse a favor—not that he'd minded stepping back from his unpredictable life for a while. Sara was supposed to be temporary. She was not his type. Hadn't been eighteen years ago and wasn't now. So why was he so drawn to her? Why did he feel more comfortable with her with every hour that passed?

He didn't search for comfort. If you fell into that trap, someone always yanked it away.

"Smells good," Sara said as she stepped into the kitchen. She was freshly scrubbed and dressed in loose pajama pants and an old T-shirt. Her hair was still slightly damp, but she'd used a blow dryer on the long dark blond strands and they looked thicker and softer than usual. Her feet were bare, and apparently she did listen to him on occasion. She wasn't wearing a bra.

He wanted her all over again.

"There's something you need to know about me," he said crisply.

Her eyebrows rose slightly. "That sounds serious."

"It is. Have a seat."

He expected an argument from her—she seemed to argue over the smallest, most unimportant things—but she took a seat at the kitchen table and lifted her face to him.

He didn't see any reason to waste time or words. "Six

years ago I got involved with a woman on the job, and she was killed."

Sara's eyes got wider. "Were you guarding her?"

"No. Serena was just there, an innocent bystander who got caught in the crossfire."

"Then it wasn't your fault. If you'd known…"

"It doesn't matter whose fault it was," Dante said, running his fingers through thick, dark strands of hair. "It happened and I wasn't there, and that's all that matters."

She stood, placing herself squarely before him. "This Serena is the past you can't leave behind."

"Yeah."

She placed a hand on his cheek. "Did you love her very much?"

His heart constricted. "I don't know," he said honestly. "Maybe. I liked her, even though she wasn't my type at all."

"What is your type?" Sara asked as her hand slipped down to the side of his neck, where her fingers came to rest over the curling end of a tattoo. She now knew it was a tip of flame that rose up on his neck, flame that also marked his shoulder. The fire tattoo surrounded a phoenix, which was so prominent on his finely shaped back. Was that phoenix symbolic? Had he risen from the ashes of his life?

"Blond, built and easy," he said crisply.

Instead of being offended, Sara smiled as her fingers traced a lick of flame. "I know you better than you know yourself, Dante Mangino. I'll bet this house and everything in it you've never even for one second thought yourself in love with a woman who was blond, built and easy. That's not really your type at all." Her smile didn't last. "You hide with women like that because they don't ask too much of you."

"Thank you, Dr. Phil," he said drily.

"I know all about hiding from life," Sara said softly. "I've been hiding for four years, so I recognize the symptoms in you."

"I don't hide from anything," Dante said.

"You don't hide from danger of the physical sort." Sara placed both of her small hands on his waist. "But you do hide. We're sleeping together, and still you keep a part of yourself from me. I'm not blind, Dante. All your talk of not staying, of not getting too involved, of me not being your type…that's hiding." She checked the timer on the oven and then directed him to sit in the chair she had recently occupied. When he was seated, she perched herself on his lap. "We have twenty minutes," she said, wrapping her arms around his neck. "Tell me about your Serena."

Chapter 8

Sara listened to the story Dante told her, and her heart broke. He *had* loved his Serena, even if he'd never admitted it to her or to himself. Her death was eating him up inside, even after all these years. He hadn't exactly been a cuddly man before meeting the math teacher—she knew that from knowing him as a teenager and from the career he had pursued—but since that time, he'd closed himself off even more staunchly than before.

Seeing Maddie Phillips's body this morning couldn't have helped matters any. She could only imagine that the sight had brought painful memories rushing back.

When the timer went off, Sara popped up, removed the casserole from the oven and placed it on the stove to cool. She immediately returned to his lap and placed her hands on his face. A harsh stubble met the softness of her palms. Even though she hated what he'd been through, even though she would've done anything to take away his pain, she was glad to know that he was capable of a deep love. No man or woman should be without it. She now believed with all her heart that it was possible to love more than once in a lifetime—but she also knew that love was rare and special, and it wasn't waiting around every corner. Some things had to be taken when they presented themselves; some things had to be claimed.

"I know what it's like to lose someone you love so much," she whispered. "But I also know that it's possible to love again."

"Don't…"

"Let me finish, please. As a matter of fact…don't say a word until I tell you I'm done. Please," she added.

He pursed his lips together, his actions obedient, his eyes defiant.

"After Robert died, I thought that was it for me. He was sick for almost a year and it was absolute hell watching him die, and when he did pass, I was depleted emotionally and physically. It was hard, and I gave up. I'd had my love, thank you very much, and I was done. One love to a customer. You've had yours and it didn't last long or end well, but them's the breaks. Besides, the pain of losing love is so horrible, who would want to go through that again? It's easier just to exist without that pain that's like no other, to live without really living at all." She leaned in and kissed Dante on the forehead, briefly, as she caught her breath. "And then you show up on my doorstep, the boy from my past turned into a fine man, and in no time at all I realize that love is not finite. The world is filled with love, and loving you doesn't take anything away from the love I felt for my husband." She smiled. "Talk about having a type. You and Robert have very little in common, and yet you're both good men with good hearts, you're both men who pursued careers that make the world a safer place." She rested her head on his shoulder. "The love I had for him is not diminished because I love you now."

She didn't expect a response in kind from Dante, but she wanted him to know how she felt.

"Are you finished?" he asked.

"For now."

"Loving me is dangerous."

"I don't care."

"I'm not going to stay. I'm not going to change my life for you or anyone else."

Sara sighed. "I don't care."

"You never struck me as a 'love for the moment' kinda gal," he said, more than a touch of sarcasm in his lowered voice.

"I'm not," she confessed. "But I'm also not a 'cut off my nose to spite my face' kinda gal." She lifted her head to look him in the eye. "I won't walk away from you to-night because you're going to break my heart tomorrow. Yes, the world is filled with love, but finding it is much too special to toss away in order to avoid the pain that comes with the end." She gave him a smile. "I guess that does make me a 'love for the moment' kinda gal."

She kissed him because a kiss was appropriate and she wanted it. He kissed her back with passion and hunger and skill, but there were no words of love. No grand declaration that she was right and he'd been a fool.

* * *

Hopped up on caffeine so maybe he could make it through the night without dozing off, Dante walked the upstairs hallway not long after Sara had retired. The area would be a lot easier to contain if the house was smaller and not quite so old. The place was impressive, but it had not been built with security in mind. It creaked at night, like an old woman whose bones were settling as she slept. Thank goodness the house had a decent alarm system.

Tomorrow he'd work on installing some extra security on the grounds. Motion detectors and cameras, to start.

Considering what had happened that day, he really should insist on moving Sara to another location. Yeah, as if she'd go for that. Odds were in a few days the crisis would be over. The matching underwear would turn out to be a coincidence. Maybe Henry Phillips had heard about the underwear thief and had decided to duplicate the crime to throw suspicion elsewhere. After all, he knew Sara's cousin Owen. Sara had kept the story out of the newspapers and off the news, but there were plenty of people who knew. Her employees, her friends, maybe even her cousin.

The problem was Henry had loved his wife. His grief was very real. They were having trouble nailing down the specifics—Henry wasn't the best when it came to remembering dates—but it was possible the underwear had been left for Maddie *before* Sara. So, where did that leave them?

Dante tried to keep his focus on the job, but that didn't work well. He'd thought Serena's story would scare Sara into realizing what she was getting herself into by being involved with him, but instead she'd gotten much more involved. Love. What a crock. Love sounded pretty but rarely worked out well, at least in his experience. Then again, a few of the men he'd worked with for so many years had found the right woman and settled down and they seemed happy enough. They were content. Even Cal. Even the Major. Dante was never content, and he wasn't sure he'd like the condition all that much.

Just after three, he crawled into bed with a sleeping Sara and gently pulled her body to his. The house was secure and his gun was close at hand. No one would get near her, not while he was there.

He wanted to wake her and strip her naked, but he didn't. She needed her sleep, and in spite of the dangers that had come into her life she looked very peaceful.

Dante didn't mean to doze off, but he got too comfortable holding Sara and he slipped into a deep and vivid dream. Serena was there. This was unlike other dreams. Here she was perched on the edge of her desk, legs crossed and one foot swaying, dark-rimmed glasses slipping down on her nose. She smiled.

"She's right, you know," Serena said.

Dante tried to stand, but he was stuck in a pupil's desk that was much too small for his body. "Right about what?" he snapped as he wrestled with the desk that held him prisoner.

Serena held up a slender finger. "One, you did love me. Deny it all you want. I know the truth. Two, you don't have any idea what your *type* is. Hello? Look at her, look at me, do the math. Men, I swear, they never know what's good for them or what they really want. Three—" a third finger popped up decisively "—what happened to me was not your fault. Not that I'm happy about it or anything, but really, no one saw it coming. Four, if you're lucky, you really do get to find love more than once. Five…"

"That's enough."

Serena leaned back on her hands. "Basically Sara was right about everything. You're lucky to have her, Dante. Don't screw it up." A wide grin grew on her face. "I like the tattoo," she said. "It's a very sweet remembrance. If only you had written me a limerick…"

He fingered the small SL that had been worked into the tribal art surrounding the dragon on his forearm. "I was drunk when I got it."

"Of course you were."

"It's not enough," he said, again trying to rise from the too-small desk. Again failing.

"You remember me," she said, the smile fading. "That's what's enough. Now, quit letting me screw with your love life. I'm starting to feel incredibly guilty. You're ruining my peaceful afterlife, so cut it out. Trust me, if you'd been the one who'd died I would've gotten a tattoo and written a limerick and cried for a while, and then I would've moved on. That's life, babe."

He felt a surge of anger. "That's life? A butcher slits your throat, and you can shrug your shoulders and say *that's life?*"

Again Serena shrugged her shoulders, and then she was gone. Dante came awake with a start and looked at the illuminated clock on the bedside table. He hadn't been asleep for more than twenty minutes, so why the vivid dream?

He crawled out of the bed, slowly and easily so as

not to wake Sara, and moved silently back into the hallway. There he leaned against the wall and closed his
eyes. Holy crap. Had he really been kidding himself all
these years about the kind of woman he liked best? He
was always drawn to the flashiest, blondest, biggest-
boobed woman in the room. If she wasn't too smart, that
was a real bonus.

But the only two women who'd ever messed with his
heart were cute and conservative, not at all flashy when
it came to their public personas. They were both scary
smart and kind deep down and just a little bit flaky—
although it seemed only he had seen that trait in them.
They were not overtly aggressive, but neither was shy
about going after what they wanted.

None of that mattered now. Keeping Sara safe was
his only priority. He wouldn't fail her. He wouldn't let
harm come near her. Dreams of Serena were hard to
take. Dreams of a slaughtered Sara would kill him.

Sara felt a bit ridiculous as she was handed off from
one man to another. She tried to come up with a scenario
to explain away Potts's presence at city hall, but he
was very obviously a bodyguard. He was also very obviously armed. Again, her usually reserved secretary
Natalie flirted and made better coffee.

It was almost a welcome distraction that afternoon
when Owen dropped in unannounced. She and her
cousin were not close. They had, in fact, butted heads
more than once in the three years since she'd returned
to Tillman. There was a certain responsibility that came
with their family name. Owen was dedicated to keeping
and making money. Sara was more interested in the

charities their family had been involved with for years. He'd been much happier when she'd been a distant relation, living in Atlanta and allowing him to run it all.

Owen talked a lot about the family name and the responsibilities that came with it, but he would never have agreed to run for mayor; there wasn't enough money in it for him.

He didn't bother with pleasantries as he burst into her office. "I am hearing the most disturbing rumors about you, Sarabeth."

The hairs on the back of her neck stood up. Very few people called her Sarabeth these days, but that was the name she'd heard whispered beneath her window, on that night when she'd been so frightened. She didn't let her alarm show. "What kind of rumors?"

He glanced at Potts, who was standing at attention on the other side of the room, silent and very, very still. "Can he wait in the outer office?"

"No," Potts responded before Sara had the chance. His low voice rumbled, leaving no room for argument.

"Fine." Owen turned his gaze to her. "You're mayor. You're a Caldwell. The people of the town look up to us, they have certain expectations, and you're shacking up with some guy you just met?"

Sara hid her outrage with a smile. "I've known Dante for years. Is there anything else?"

Owen nodded to Potts. "Who's the goon?"

Was it her imagination, or did Potts growl low in his throat?

"I'm afraid there's been some unpleasant excitement in my life lately," she explained. "Dante thought a bodyguard wouldn't be a bad idea."

"What kind of excitement calls for armed muscle?" Owen snapped.

Sara had had enough. "Did you hear about Maddie Phillips?"

"Yes." He paled a little. "What does that have to do with you?"

She thought of that whispered "Sarabeth" and stalled. "The details aren't important." She narrowed her eyes. "You dated Maddie, didn't you?"

He looked down at her desk, seeming to study an arrangement of pens there. "Yeah, for the three days she and Henry weren't together."

Sara remembered. In a small town the love lives of others was always of interest, and there were few, if any, secrets. "They had a fight and broke up, and you moved in on her before the day was over."

"It wasn't serious," he said.

Not for Maddie, she suspected. She wasn't so sure about Owen. "She was a good ten years younger than you."

"Age is not important," her cousin argued. "Wasn't your husband several years older than you?"

She paled. He really had no right to bring Robert into this, but Owen had never cared about the old courtesy of not hitting below the belt. She took some comfort from knowing that Dante could make mincemeat of this little man with a glance.

"I was just thinking that you must be distraught about her death, that's all," she explained.

He looked a little guilty. "Yeah. She was a sweet girl."

Sara tried to imagine her cousin taking underwear from the clothesline, buying replacements, leaving them on the porch…taking a knife to Maddie Phillips. None of it seemed to fit. If nothing else, he would be horrified to be caught and labeled an underwear thief. Appearance was everything to Owen. Appearance and money. If he wanted someone dead he'd probably hire the dirty work out.

Owen tried to change the subject. "I didn't come here to talk about Maddie Phillips. I came to talk about you. Why is this Dante character living in your house? For God's sake, Sara, you can get laid without letting the entire town know about it."

"I beg your pardon?" she snapped.

"You're a grown woman, I know that, but when you get an itch, can't you at least be discreet about getting it scratched?"

Sara stood slowly, and Owen reacted by taking a small step back. Potts snickered. At least, it sounded a little like a snicker. "We're related through our fathers, and unfortunately I can't do a damn thing about that." Her voice remained even and calm. "If you want to know more about my security detail and the reasons for it, I'll be happy to sit down and tell you all about it. But my private life is none of your business. If that's what you came here to talk about, you can leave. Now."

"Watch your step," Owen said sharply as he moved toward the door. "You're a public figure, Sara. You're a Caldwell. Don't forget that." He slammed the door behind him.

"Putz," Potts said softly.

Sara didn't say so, but she had to agree.

Owen's last words stayed with her, and she

realized how much she had always hated them, not just from him but from most of her family. *A B in math isn't good enough, Sarabeth. You're a Caldwell. You can't date that Mangino boy, Sarabeth. He's just not suitable. Remember, you're a Caldwell. You have to run for mayor, Sara. You're a Caldwell. People expect it of you.*

She wished she had the courage to run away, but she hadn't been able to run at seventeen, and dammit, she couldn't run now.

Jesse apparently thought one day was enough time for Dante to come to his senses and agree to return to his duties. He seemed almost surprised to be denied, but not surprised enough to stalk away.

They sat in Sara's parlor and talked about the case. The ABI—Alabama Bureau of Investigation—had sent in seasoned investigators, which was a huge help. Jesse would remain involved, though. How could he not? This was the first murder in Tillman in more than fifteen years, and it had happened on his watch. He wasn't happy about that.

Sure enough, their picture was in the thin Tillman paper, front page above the fold. They had made the Huntsville and the Birmingham papers, too, although not as prominently.

Dante didn't have anything to add to Jesse's skimpy news about the murder investigation. There had been no prints found on the underwear that had been left for Sara, or on the box. Dante had the team there, looking into where those particular brands could be purchased. With any luck they could trace the purchases and find

the man who'd made them. Judging by the luck they'd
had so far, that wasn't likely.

So, how long was he going to be stuck here, living
with Sara, sleeping with her, waiting for her to be at-
tacked? He was already wound so tight he was about to
pop. A few more days of this and he'd be unbearable.
A few more weeks, and he'd be a basket case.

Dante never lost his cool, but he was coming damn
close to doing just that.

After a short visit where they exchanged information, he kicked Jesse out, making it clear that his cousin
was not forgiven for his latest stunt and then promising
to stop by the Little League game tomorrow afternoon,
if he could. Opal left early with plans to have supper with
her son, Elliott, but as usual she left a casserole in the
fridge.

Sara got home a little after four, a smiling Hawkins
in tow. It didn't take long to find out why Hawkins was
grinning. Apparently Potts had a date with Sara's secretary, Natalie, and had rushed back to the hotel to grab
a shower and change clothes. Potts never rushed.

Hawkins checked the perimeter of the house, leaving
Dante and Sara alone. Immediately, Sara began to do a
striptease. Shoes were kicked off, her jacket was discarded and a couple of buttons of her conservative
blouse came undone.

Unfortunately for him, that's where it stopped.

He wanted out. He hurt already. He never should've
come back to Tillman, favor or no favor.

"My cousin Owen stopped by this afternoon," she
said. The expression on her face made her feelings for
her cousin more than clear.

"I remember him. Is he still a prick?"

"Yes," she said without hesitation. "He wants you out of the house."

"Interesting." Her anonymous caller wanted the same thing. "Would there be any reason for Owen to harass you? Any payoff if he scared you into running or hiding?" If she died, did Owen get all the family money? There weren't many Caldwells left, he knew that. Not many Caldwells, and no more Vances from her husband's branch of the family. How much would Owen inherit if something happened to Sara? He didn't ask that question, but he would find out.

"No," Sara said, answering the questions he had asked aloud. "He's just an annoying little man who can't stand for anyone else to be happy."

He should tell Sara that he needed some space. They needed to cool things off for a while and concentrate on business.

His cell rang, saving him from going there, and he snagged it. "Mangino."

He was not surprised to hear Murphy on the line. "Man, I don't think we're going to have any luck with your underwear," Bennings' resident geek said. "The pieces were made especially for a specialty store called Lucy's Lingerie. Heard of it?"

"Yeah." Who hadn't? Lucy's was a chain that had a store in every decent-size mall in the southeast. They also had a Web site. It was slightly less than a month past Valentine's Day. Even if they were able to get their hands on a list of men who'd purchased the correct styles in the correct sizes with their credit cards, it wouldn't help much. The list would not include cash purchases, and Dante had a feeling their guy wasn't sloppy enough to use his charge card. If he left no prints, there would be no paper trail, either.

"We'll keep looking into it," Murphy said, "but I don't think we should hold out much hope. But hey, I do have some good news." The geek's voice was suddenly downright cheery.

"I could use some good news," Dante said.

"Kelly and I are getting married."

Dante paused a moment before saying, "No joke? Why?"

"Thank you for those warm, heartfelt congratulations," Murphy said wryly.

"That doesn't answer my question," Dante said, turning around so Sara wouldn't see his face.

"I'll assume you mean the second question, the why."

"Yeah."

Leave it to Murphy to get right to the point without getting mushy. "She's the one for me. Cal's sister or not, Kelly is it."

"You sound as if you're playing tag," Dante grumbled.

"Does that mean you won't be my best man?"

Was he kidding? "Shouldn't you just, like, elope and get it over with?"

"Kelly wants a real wedding, and what Kelly wants Kelly gets."

Another man down. "When?"

"The second weekend in June."

"I think I'm busy that weekend," Dante grumbled.

"Clear your calendar, bud, I want to see you in a tux, and I expect a kick-ass best man speech from you."

"I'll think about it." He ended the call abruptly, and

only then did he realize that Sara had been listening to every word.

"Your friend is getting married?" she asked with a smile.

He supposed his question about eloping had given it away. "Yeah, poor bastard."

She laughed and walked toward him slowly, those hips he loved swaying. How he would love to see her in that hidden long, swishy skirt or the red dress instead of those manly trousers. How he longed to see her with her hair down and loose, instead of caught up in a matronly bun. He wanted her to be free of the restrictions she'd placed on herself, but how could he ask that of her when he was living with so many restrictions of his own?

"Poor bastard?"

Dante slapped himself on the forehead. "Kelly must be pregnant. Murphy has no choice but to marry her. Cal would kill him otherwise."

"Pregnancy is the only reason for marriage?" she asked lightly, seeing right through him.

"When the woman in question is Quinn Calhoun's sister, it's definitely a reason. Marriage or death. What a dilemma." He remembered Murphy's sappy words. *Kelly is it.* If he had an it, if he *wanted* an it, Sara could be the one. Not the staid mayor who always did what everyone expected her to do, but the woman who was giving in bed, who spoke her mind even when he didn't want to hear, who danced in the kitchen when she thought no one was looking, who burned mismatched socks and arranged wildflowers in expensive vases and who asked nothing of him…and at the same time asked for everything.

More than anything else, he longed to see her wrapped around him, naked and too lost in the heat they generated to think of asking personal questions and dissecting his pitiful love life. He wanted to hear her moan low in her throat the way she did just before she came, and he wanted to feel the quiver that commanded her body.

He wouldn't be asking her to cool it tonight. He was too selfish to let her go just yet, too needy to be noble and end it neatly and quickly. Maybe his love life was pitiful, but his sex life was just fine.

Chapter 9

The weekend passed as smoothly as possible, given the current state of affairs. When Monday came again Sara's days fell into an easy routine, not all that different from what they'd been like before Dante had arrived to turn her life upside down. She spent her weekdays at the office, arguing with Len Cleaver about whether or not the six rusting cars in his yard violated a city ordinance; working with the comptroller to find more money for salaries; having frequent meetings with her capable vice mayor, the elder Harlan Peabody; answering the stack of mail that never got any smaller; and fending off Tillman residents who wanted one favor or another. She attended a spring concert at the local high school and managed not to cringe when the clarinets squeaked their way through one of her favorite classical pieces.

She had lunch with Patty and Lydia a time or two, but instead of meeting at a local restaurant, as usual, they brought something into the office under Potts's careful watch. He did, at least, agree to leave the three women alone while they ate. Of course he agreed. That meant he got to spend time in the outer office with Natalie.

Even though she had been leery of the constant guard, she got accustomed to Potts and Hawkins very quickly. They were professional and unobtrusive, and the budding romance between Natalie and Potts was amusing and sweet—and gave her friends something to talk about besides Dante. She would not have thought the big bald man was capable of blushing so completely, but whenever Natalie walked into the room, he did.

She had not thought Natalie was capable of smiling constantly and learning to make a consistently decent pot of coffee, but that's what was happening.

Dante slept during the day, spent his nights making love to her and then keeping watch, and in his spare hours he made phone calls and studied case files and checked the Internet for one thing or another. He thought it was a possibility that someone Robert had prosecuted in Atlanta was behind the crimes, even though it had been four years since Robert's death and three years since her move back to Tillman, even though he could not come up with any way to connect Maddie Phillips to that scenario.

She hadn't thought anyone from her past as an assistant district attorney's wife would be able to find her, not easily, but Dante showed her how very easy it could be. He typed her name into a people-finder search engine, and two minutes later he had her current address. In three minutes he had a map to her house. That was just as scary as hearing her name whispered in the dead of night.

The sex was fabulous and frequent, and while sometimes it seemed that Dante was as swept away by what they'd found as she was, she was aware that he always held something of himself back from her. Even when they were naked and joined, he didn't open up entirely. Even when they threw everything else to the wind, he kept the wall he'd erected between them solid and strong. There were moments when she was certain that wall was thicker and stronger than it had been in the early days, as if he had backed away from her at the same time he'd moved so close.

And still, she was happy most of the time. She was happier than she'd been in years. They danced in the parlor. He cooked for her. She rubbed his back and studied each and every tattoo. One night he pointed out to her the small SL that was worked into the artwork surrounding his dragon tattoo, almost as if he expected its presence would scare her away. It didn't. His pain, what he called his failure, proved that he was human, that he felt deeply. He saw that as a failing. She did not.

He had marked the passages of his life on his body. In the phoenix that covered one shoulder and crawled up his neck; in a smaller tattoo that marked his time with the Marines. It was days before she discovered that her own initials—SLC—were well hidden within one wing of the phoenix. She thought about asking him about those initials, but was afraid that too much discussion at this point would send him running. She wasn't ready to give him up. Not yet. Maybe never.

She was even becoming accustomed to the scars that marred the perfection of his body. Like his tattoos, there weren't many of them. Like his tattoos, they marked passages of his life. It had taken her some time to be comfortable enough to touch them all, to ask about the wheres and hows of each injury. She had kissed the horrid scar that was a result of the time he'd been shot, and as she'd kissed it she'd been very careful to hide her tears.

Lying in bed on a Saturday night two weeks after they'd become lovers, a little more than a week after Maddie Phillips had been killed, she traced the dragon on his forearm with her fingertip. Hawkins had gone home a couple of hours ago, dismissed by Dante. Ten minutes later they'd been there, in her bed. They were sweaty and spent, hearts beating hard and bodies still shaking. She was content. Dante was as content as he ever allowed himself to be.

"How long is this going to last?" she asked, breaking the silence that stretched between them.

He turned his head to look at her, a dark question in his dark eyes.

"The constant guard," she clarified. She honestly didn't want to know how long he thought their relationship would last. "Nothing's happened since Maddie's murder. How long can I justify having 'round-the-clock bodyguards?"

"Until I say it's no longer necessary."

He seemed very sure of himself, but in many ways she was more practical than he was. She always had been.

Once she'd let the pain of losing Dante go and gotten on with her life, once she'd met Robert and allowed herself to be happy with him, she hadn't given Dante Mangino a lot of thought. Some, of course, but not a lot. She'd almost lost her virginity to him. Would have, if a sheriff's deputy hadn't come across their parking place when he had and nearly scared the life out of them with a tap on the window. He'd sent them home and they'd gone, and even though they'd been interrupted at a very bad time, they'd thought themselves lucky to get off so easily.

But it hadn't been so easy, after all. Naturally that deputy had known her grandfather and had spilled the beans the very next day. Her Papa wouldn't stand for his little girl becoming a woman in the backseat of any boy's car. And Dante Mangino, long haired and irreverent, would not do *at all.*

They'd basically run him out of town. Threats had been issued—threats that had ranged from jail to a good old-fashioned beating for Dante to sending Sarabeth to a private school many, many miles away. Dante hadn't allowed himself to be intimidated, but Sara had known her Papa was capable of carrying out his threats. Every single one. Eventually, knowing he had no choice but to leave, Dante had asked her to run away with him. She'd declined. Even then she'd been practical, she'd known that what they had was heat, not stability.

She had loved him, there was no doubt about that. She'd wanted him to stay in Tillman, to face her grandfather down and convince the old man that he was wrong about them. She'd wanted Dante to cut his hair and go to Tillman High and make good grades and play on the football team and become what he was not. She'd wanted Dante to prove to her grandfather that he was a better man than the old man believed, and she'd wanted to see if the heat they generated would turn into something more.

Most of all, she'd wanted him to fight for her. Instead he'd left town, just as her grandfather had ordered.

Looking back she realized she hadn't just wanted him to fight for her, she'd wanted him to *change* for her. Now she was old enough to know that people didn't change, not really. More, she knew she didn't want Dante to change.

How many nights had she wished she'd jumped on Dante's motorcycle and taken off with him when he'd asked? Where would they be now if she had?

In just a little while he'd leave her here to sleep while he kept watch. It was beginning to seem silly that he insisted on staying awake all night when he could be right here, sleeping with her. On the one occasion she'd said as much to Dante, he'd reminded her of Maddie Phillips's death. He'd only had to do that once.

If Dante didn't believe that her life was in danger, would he still be here? Or would he already have left her behind, just as he'd left her eighteen years ago?

She shook that thought off. Now that she was older, she realized that she had been the one to leave him first, and he'd known it all along.

Dante was making his famous chili for supper. There was nothing wrong with Opal's cooking, but he was getting damn tired of casseroles. Tuna casserole, chicken casserole, ham casserole—after a while it all started to taste the same. He understood the convenience of tossing the ingredients of a well-balanced meal into a pot with a sauce or a can of soup, but he was in the mood for some red meat. He was most especially in the mood for a meal that didn't have a green pea or a carrot square anywhere in sight.

He actually liked to cook, now and then. He'd never make a chef, but there was something therapeutic about chopping onions and garlic and going wild with the spices. He had always loved stirring the pot.

In the past few days he'd become very aware that things could not continue as they were for much longer. There were no more clues in the Maddie Phillips murder, and there had been no more phone calls for Sara, no more gifts or thefts or disturbances outside her window. The man responsible could just be waiting for Dante to leave, as he would before too much longer.

What if he left and the next day Sara's body was found, bloodied and abandoned as Maddie's had been? What if he stayed on indefinitely, guarding her with his life, keeping her from harm...falling in love with her when he knew he should not?

He hadn't dreamed about Serena in days, and lately he had been able to think of her without feeling a surge of rage. She wasn't Sara. What had happened to her wasn't his fault. He would've saved her if he could; he would've given his life for hers. But he hadn't been given that choice.

So, where did that leave him?

Sara walked up behind him and slipped her arms around his waist. "Smells good," she said softly.

He liked the feel of her weight and warmth as she held him, and he knew what he felt was more than the sex, more than the physical need she filled so well. "It's just chili."

"I haven't had chili in ages."

Suddenly he knew what he had to do. The solution was so right, he didn't know why he hadn't thought of it before. "Let's leave here, tonight," he said simply.

Sara's body stiffened and drew slightly away from his. "You want to…go somewhere?" she asked. "Like a vacation?"

"No. We leave here and we don't ever come back."

She gave a nervous laugh. "You're kidding me, right? I can't possibly just pack up and leave. I'm mayor. I have responsibilities with the city and with a number of family enterprises that I can't abandon on a whim."

Dante felt everything in his body tighten. "Your panty thief is very patient, and I can't stay here forever."

"Why not?" she asked, her voice quick and low. "You could ask Jesse for your job back. The police department could certainly use you, and I'm certain he'd say yes. You can live here as long as you want." He heard the longing in her voice, and knew it was what she wanted. Him, babies, marriage—the whole traditional deal.

Some things never changed. He wanted her to run away with him and start fresh somewhere else and she wouldn't do it. She wanted him to change who he was to stay here with her.

Dante Mangino, family man and cop. No way.

He would never admit that it hurt to be refused again. He wasn't seventeen, wasn't a kid foolish enough to wear his heart on his sleeve. But yeah, it hurt. He turned down the heat on the stove and then turned to face Sara.

He gave her a smile. "Seems like old times. You can't go and I can't stay. Doesn't matter." He took her chin in his hand. "We knew all along this was temporary." Surely he didn't have to tell her that it was over.

Stupid, stupid, stupid.

Sara stared at the stack of papers in front of her. She'd decided to work at home that afternoon. Though she hadn't told anyone so, it had seemed that the walls of her office at city hall had been closing in on her, and she'd found herself on the verge of a frustrated scream more than once. Now she was closed in her home office, making no progress at all on the job before her. Hawkins stood guard on the other side of the door. He didn't like the arrangement much, and had only agreed to it after checking the single window in the room to make sure it was securely locked. Dante slept upstairs, as he often did in the afternoon before she got home.

Stupid, stupid, stupid. The accusatory words went through her mind again. She had felt the change in Dante the moment she'd refused to leave town with him. It didn't make sense to run and hide; that wasn't the way she did things. Why couldn't he just stay here with her? Stubborn man.

He hadn't come to her bed or invited her into his since that encounter over chili four days ago. Not once. He hadn't kissed her, hadn't so much as touched her, and when she'd been foolish and optimistic enough to make a move on him he'd cut her down with a cold and unyielding expression on his hard and beautiful face.

To those around them, everything between them probably appeared to be the same. Dante remained in her house, he drove her to work, and he was as protective as always. He just didn't end his nights in her arms, and that broke her heart.

Why hadn't she said yes when he'd asked her to leave with him? The city of Tillman could survive without her. The police department would survive without Dante. All her family responsibilities could be handed over to Opal and Owen. Life would go on, the world wouldn't crumble. So why had she so quickly and certainly refused him?

She was afraid, dammit. She was more afraid of leaving everything she knew than she was of facing a murderer. What did that say about her? Had she become so sensible, so afraid of adventure—so afraid of life— that she was literally hiding herself away in Tillman?

Sara heard familiar voices arguing on the other side of the door. Hawkins and Opal. She couldn't make out every word, but she heard a "You can't" and a sharp "Young man!" That made her smile. Opal apparently won the argument, since a moment later there was a brief knock and the door opened to Opal carrying a silver tea service.

"I thought you might like some tea," Opal said, patently ignoring the glowering young man who held the door for her. "I made some oatmeal-raisin cookies, too."

There was plenty of room on the desk for the tea service, and Opal placed the heavy silver there. The cookies smelled heavenly. Sara smiled at her bodyguard for the afternoon. She couldn't help but think that if Potts was still on duty, the argument would still be going on. "Would you like some of these oatmeal-raisin cookies?" she asked.

"No, thank you, ma'am," Hawkins responded sharply.

"They're very good," Sara said, trying to tempt him.

Hawkins shook his head. Apparently she couldn't tempt anyone with anything these days.

Opal smiled tightly. "He doesn't know what's good."

Hawkins responded, "I don't like raisins in my cookies." He grimaced. "Tastes like bugs."

"And you would know what bugs taste like," Opal said sharply, her false smile gone.

Sara heard Dante's footsteps on the stairway before she caught sight of him heading for her office. He was rumpled with sleep and obviously annoyed. By his normal schedule, he should have another hour before waking for the night.

These days his nights were spent roaming dark hallways and investigating one thing or another on the Internet. He didn't sleep while she did. He didn't come to her bed.

God, she missed him.

In his presence, the argument about raisins tasting like bugs ended. Opal and Hawkins both looked contrite. Standing in the doorway, Dante ignored them and pinned his sleepy eyes on hers. "We have a lead on your anonymous call."

"Really?" she said, surprised. "After all this time?" They had traced the blocked call back to a disposable cell, one of those cheap phones that could be bought in any convenience store.

"Maybe. It took awhile, I know, but it looks as if Murphy has it narrowed down to a particular batch, anyway. Maybe we can find out where it was purchased. Can't hurt." He gave her a decidedly unfriendly and even chilly smile.

It was so obvious that he wanted out. Out of her

house, out of her life. He was still here because he felt obligated, because he didn't want to fail her the way he'd failed his Serena.

But that wasn't going to last forever.

Ask me again, she thought, trying to communicate to Dante silently that a part of her wanted to leave with him. To disappear, to start over… It could be heaven, if she allowed it to be.

But instead of hearing her thoughts he turned away and headed for the kitchen, where he'd make coffee and raid the refrigerator.

When Opal and Hawkins were once again gone and the door had been closed behind them, Sara placed her forehead on the desk and took a deep breath just to keep from crying.

He couldn't stay here anymore. It was time to leave, past time to leave, and yet he couldn't make himself go. He'd make other arrangements by the weekend. He'd bring in more Bennings agents, install more security, get Sara a gun and teach her how to use it….

Dante was in the spare bedroom, which was now entirely his, seated at a small desk with his laptop open and glowing before him. The investigation was moving slowly, but it was moving. Lots of underwear exactly like those left for Maddie Phillips and for Sara had been sold, but Maddie wore an odd size, and they had been able to find a store in Birmingham that had sold the two right styles in the two right sizes on the same day.

Which meant the perv had targeted Sara and Maddie both from the start. This wasn't coincidence; it wasn't random.

His head snapped up when one of the motion detector lights in the backyard came on. For a moment he sat there and listened. In the past few days dogs and raccoons had set off the lights a number of times. Still, he listened for any sound that shouldn't be there. In a few minutes the light would go off, unless there was continued activity in the range of the motion detector.

The light went off. All was quiet, inside and outside. Down the hall Sara slept, and just knowing she was there tore him up in ways he couldn't deal with right now.

He had to get out.

A soft noise from downstairs caught his attention. He glanced through the open doorway into the hall and realized that the night-lights Sara had everywhere were no longer burning. A glance at his computer, which offered the only light in the room, showed that it was now running on battery.

Someone had cut the power.

Dante stood as another noise, louder this time, echoed up the stairway.

Chapter 10

Sara woke with a start to find Dante standing beside her bed, gun in hand.

"What's…" She had been about to say "happening" but an unexpected sound interrupted her. It was a thump and a scrape, as if someone had bumped into a piece of furniture downstairs.

She tossed back the covers and rolled out of bed as Dante put a silencing finger to his lips. Together they walked to the bedroom doorway, where they stopped and strained to listen. Sure enough, there was another shuffle. The sound might have come from the kitchen. It was difficult to tell from here.

"Lock the door behind me," Dante whispered. "Don't open it for anyone but me. Call Jesse and tell him there's an intruder in the house."

Sara nodded, and as Dante slipped into the hallway

she did as he'd instructed, leaning against the locked door and listening as hard as she could. Listening and praying. After what couldn't have been more than a few seconds she ran for her bedside phone and lifted the receiver. There was no dial tone. She didn't waste any time before digging into her purse for her cell phone, but as she flipped it open the words No Signal stared back at her, even though she'd never before had any trouble getting a connection here.

No landline, no cell phone. The computer, which was connected to the Internet by Wi-Fi, was her only hope for reaching out to anyone. Her computer was downstairs in her office, but Dante usually had a laptop set up in his bedroom. Still, would it do her any good? It wasn't likely that the police chief would be checking his e-mail at one in the morning.

Sara ran back to the door and pressed her ear to the wood, straining to listen and again, saying a silent prayer. It didn't seem that she could do much of anything else.

Dante eased his way down the stairs. The alarm had not sounded, which meant that either the intruder had the alarm code or it had been disabled. Only Opal, Potts and Hawkins had the new code, he'd made sure of that, so he was betting that the system had been tampered with by someone who knew what he was doing.

Again, he heard a soft noise from the kitchen.

Gun in hand, Dante made his way toward the kitchen. The sounds were so soft, if he'd been sleeping, he never would have heard a thing. Sara sometimes said he was being too cautious, staying awake and alert during the night hours, but in this business there was no such thing as being too cautious. When it came to Sara's life, he could not be too careful.

He looked down a narrow hallway and through the doorway. The kitchen door that opened into the backyard stood wide-open, letting in a bit of light from a neighbor's distant floodlights. The figure of a man was silhouetted near that open door. The intruder opened and closed a drawer without even looking into it. His eyes were on the entrance to the room, as if he were waiting for Dante to appear. Dante eased down the hallway without making a sound, staying in the shadows for as long as possible. His own night vision was very good, which might give him an advantage over the man who had broken into Sara's house. Another step or two, though, and he'd be in plain sight.

The moment the intruder saw Dante standing there, he turned and sprinted through the open kitchen door. Dante fired one warning shot, then took off after the man. If this was the SOB who'd killed Maddie Phillips and terrorized Sara, he wanted him dead. If he was a common thief, he'd be content with kicking the crap out of him.

A common thief who cut the power and disabled the alarm system. Unlikely.

The man was fast, taking off through Sara's backyard and into another as if he knew his way around the neighborhood even in the dark. The runner's strides were long and fast, confident in the surroundings. A nearby fretful dog began to bark. A neighbor, probably alarmed by the gunshot, turned on a back porch light. Dante listened for the sirens that would indicate Jesse was on his way, but heard nothing other than the dog's

bark and the sound of his own feet pounding on the
ground.

He was gaining on the intruder, who ran across a
deserted street and into the neighborhood park, which
was naturally deserted at this time of night. In a larger
city it might've been a haunt for gangs or drug dealers,
but not here. Never here.

The light from a streetlamp gave Dante his first real
look at the man who'd broken into Sara's house. The
man was thirtyish, thin and had short hair of an indis-
tinguishable color. As they moved deeper into the park,
the man turned on Dante and pulled a gun.

A gunshot fired, but it went wild as the shooter continued to run backward and not take the time to properly
aim at his target. As a precautionary measure, Dante hit
the ground and rolled away. The bullet zinged past,
coming much too close for comfort.

On the hard, chilled ground, Dante lay still for a moment, assessing the situation—judging where the opponent was, how fast he was moving, what direction he
was headed in. He took a firmer grip on his own gun.

The man who'd broken into Sara's house apparently
thought Dante was down because he stopped running
away and eased back toward his opponent. Fool. Maybe
he thought he'd found his target and he was coming
back to finish the job. His gun seemed ready enough.

Dante waited a moment, until the shooter was close
enough to suit him and then he rolled onto his back,
swung his gun up and fired, all in one smooth motion.
Since he wanted to talk to this man and find out what
the hell was going on, he aimed for, and hit, the knee.

The intruder screamed and dropped his gun as he fell

to the ground. Dante stood and, after kicking the fallen weapon away, looked down at the screaming man in disgust. "Hurts like hell, doesn't it?"

"Yes!" the man screamed. "Call an ambulance! Get me a doctor! Oh, my God, it *hurts!*"

"Bullets have a tendency to do that." Dante dropped down to his haunches for a better look at the man. He didn't look evil. No, he looked like an ordinary man. He was too thin and his nose had been broken at least once. "What's your name?"

"What difference does it make?" the man screamed. "I'm wounded!"

Dante felt no sympathy. "Well, when you run around at night, breaking into people's houses and shooting at them, that tends to happen."

"Help me!"

"I don't think so. Not unless you help me first."

After a moment there was a hoarse shout from the man on the ground. "It wasn't my idea!"

Again, Dante listened for the sound of sirens and heard none. True, time often got messed up when the adrenaline was pumping, but Jesse and others should be well on their way by now.

"Whose idea was it?" he asked.

"She'll kill me if I tell!"

Dante very calmly pressed the muzzle of his gun to the man's good knee, and he left it there for a long, silent moment. *She.* Strange. "I won't kill you, sport. Not yet, anyway."

The fallen man stared at the gun, took several shallow, panicked breaths, and then he screamed, "Mama! It was my mama! She came up with the whole plan on her own.

I never did like it much, but she was so sure it would work and she nagged me about it until I agreed."

The hairs on the back of Dante's neck bristled. "Mama? What the hell is your name, boy, and I swear, if you don't answer me right now…"

"Elliott," the sobbing man said. "My name is Elliott Greenwood."

Opal's son.

Unable to get a signal on her cell phone or a dial tone on her landline, Sara stood at the doorway with her ear pressed to the wood. She listened. For a few minutes she heard nothing more than the faint sounds from the first floor, but soon she heard a shout and pounding footsteps and then a gunshot followed by more noise—then silence.

She ran to the window and looked down on the front yard, but all was still there. If the intruder and Dante had left by the kitchen door, they'd be in the backyard. She couldn't see the backyard from here, but she did have a view, of sorts, from the other window in her room, a small window that overlooked the side yard.

Moving quickly, Sara threw open the window, pushed at the screen until it popped out and stuck her head through the opening, craning to see into the rear yard. Sure enough, a figure of a man ran catty-corner into Mrs. Wilson's yard. Dante's figure, more easily recognizable to her, followed. She breathed a sigh of relief, happy to see with her own eyes that he had not been shot.

The two men soon disappeared into the darkness, leaving Sara alone in a too-dark, too-quiet house. She flipped the switch to turn on the overhead light, but nothing happened. She didn't really think that the bulb had burned out, but just in case she checked her bedside lamp. Nothing. No wonder she hadn't been able to get a dial tone! All the phones in her house were portable, which meant they needed electricity to work. As soon as this was over, she was getting an old-fashioned phone that would function with nothing but a landline.

That plan didn't help her at all at the moment. She'd have to go to a neighbor's house to call Jesse. Since she'd seen the intruder run, with Dante right behind him, it should be safe enough to leave the room where he'd left her with strict instructions to stay.

She would not sit here while Dante was in trouble, not if she could call in the cavalry.

Even though she'd seen the intruder leave, she stood at the closed and locked door for a moment, gathering her courage. No power. No phone. No cell phone. Just her, an empty house and a burning need to get help.

Sara left her post at the door to pull on her bathrobe and step into the slippers that rested halfway beneath her bed. Dante needed help. He needed her to do this, no matter how scary it might be.

The bedroom door whispered a creak as she opened it, giving her a start even though she knew it sometimes made that noise even on a good day. For a moment she stood in the doorway, listening and planning. Down the stairs, to the front door and out, and to the Kingman house next door. Judson sometimes stayed up late, so maybe he'd be alert and she wouldn't have to waste time waiting for someone coherent to answer the doorbell.

She took the steps carefully, knowing that to rush down the stairs in the dark was not wise. She wouldn't do Dante any good if she was lying at the foot of the stairs with a twisted ankle, or worse. As she reached the bottom of the stairway she heard a noise that made her stomach turn and her heart dance. Maybe it was a step, maybe it was a shuffle—but she was not alone in this house.

Sara stood very still. If she could see little in the darkness, the same would be true of this second intruder. Her eyes flicked to the front door, which was accentuated by the light from a streetlamp seeping through the narrow floor-to-ceiling panes of glass on either side. It wasn't all that far from the foot of the stairway to the front entrance. Through the foyer, around one chair and a table, and she'd be there. This was a big house, so even if the intruder heard her, by the time he got there she'd be gone. Once the door was open she'd run and she would not look back.

She took a step toward the door, trying not to make a sound. Was it too late for that? What if the man in her house had heard the bedroom door squeak and was waiting in the shadows for her? What if he'd heard her light tread on the stairs and was waiting to grab her as she made her way to the door? Sara held her breath as she took another step. It would be so easy to be paralyzed with fear. It would be so easy to creep back up the stairs to her bedroom, where she'd lock and close the door and crawl under the covers to wait for Dante.

Leaving him entirely on his own, without the help he thought was coming. No, she couldn't do that to him.

She heard another noise, and realized with a ribbon of fear in her blood that the noise came from upstairs.

That was it. She ran for the front door, reaching for the dead bolt with trembling fingers. She held her breath and muttered a curse when the dead bolt refused to give. Damn old house! Finally the lock turned with a loud click.

She was stopped from flinging open the door by a familiar voice and the dancing beam of a flashlight.

"Sara? Sara, honey, is that you?"

She turned to see Opal walking cautiously down the stairs, flashlight in one hand. Even in the dim light the woman's form was recognizable. Sara had never been so relieved to see anyone in her life.

And then the most obvious question popped into her mind. "What are you doing here?"

Opal reached the bottom of the stairway. "Judson Kingman called me. He said he saw someone walking around the backyard, messing with things that shouldn't be messed with, and he wanted to see if it was one of your bodyguards checking things out. He said the man didn't look familiar, so he wanted to check. He tried to call you but didn't get an answer, so he was alarmed."

Thank God for nosy neighbors! "Did he call the police?"

"No, I told him I'd check things out for myself first. No need to get everyone riled up over nothing."

"Nothing?" Sara stepped away from the front door. "Hardly. A man disabled the alarm system, cut the power and broke into the house. I heard a gunshot!"

"Oh, dear. Where is the intruder now?" Opal sounded genuinely alarmed.

"Dante chased him. I watched out the window and saw them running southeast. I need to call Jesse, but the phones are worthless and my cell isn't getting a signal."

Opal reached into the deep pocket of her shapeless

dress. "Let me try 9-1-1 on mine." When she opened the flip phone the light from the dial illuminated her face. She pressed three buttons and raised the phone to her ear. "This is Opal Greenwood. I'm at 225 Maple Street. There's an intruder. Please send the police immediately." She nodded once and ended the call.

Sara reached out. Her hand still trembled. "Can I borrow your phone? I told Dante that I'd call Jesse and tell him what was going on."

Opal hesitated, and then she handed over the cell phone. "Of course. Why not?"

Sara gave the phone her attention, flipping it open and staring down at the plain background and the words No Signal.

Her head snapped up, and she realized that Opal now held a small gun, as well as a flashlight. "Nifty little device, the cell signal blocker. I ordered it off the Internet." She smiled. "Lovely invention, the Internet."

Sara took a step back, once again gauging the distance to the door and escape. Opal raised the gun, holding it steady, and aimed at Sara's head. "Oh, no, Mrs. Vance," she said, a new coldness in her voice. "Let's wait right here, shall we?"

Chapter 11

Dante reached into the pocket of his jeans and snagged his cell phone. Jesse, who was accustomed to being awakened in the middle of the night, answered before the second ring.

"Edwards."

"I'm in a park not too far from Sara's house with a wounded Elliott Greenwood. He broke into Sara's house tonight."

"Elliott Greenwood? Opal's son?" Jesse sounded suddenly alert.

"Yeah."

Elliott screamed, "Tell him to send an ambulance! I'm dying, here!"

"You're not dying," Dante said without sympathy.

"Is that Elliott?" Jesse asked.

"Yep. I kinda shot him in the knee."

"Great," Jesse growled.

Elliott had collapsed to the ground and was sobbing softly.

"I'm going to bind his hands behind his back with his belt..." Dante explained, knowing with the busted knee and his hands immobile Elliiot wouldn't be able to do much more than flop around like a fish out of water, "...while I go check on Sara."

"Is she hurt?"

"No. She's waiting in her bedroom until I get back."

"Then you stay with Elliott until either I or the paramedics get there. It'll just be a few minutes."

"I don't work for you anymore," Dante said without anger.

"No, you don't. I'm asking you as a cousin. As a friend. Don't leave the suspect bound and bleeding in the park."

He didn't like the idea but agreed, knowing someone would be there very soon.

Dante sat on the ground beside the sobbing Elliott. He really wanted to ask about Maddie Phillips, but it wasn't his place and might even end up damaging whatever case Jesse could put together. Was Elliott a pervert and a murderer or just a burglar? He'd said it was "Mama's plan" and Dante couldn't see the woman who made him pancakes being involved with her son's sexual perversion and senseless murder. Maybe there was some valuables in the house that she wanted. It was sad that even the seemingly best among humankind could turn out to be crooked and selfish.

Elliott let out a strangled cry.

"Don't be a baby," Dante said. "You're wounded, not dying. If I'd wanted to kill you, you'd be dead already."

"It really hurts."

"That's the point."

What kind of a man allowed his mother to plan burglaries for him? It was sick, that's for sure. It also didn't make any sense. Sara would gladly give Opal anything she asked for. If she wanted the silver teapot or the painting on the dining-room wall or anything else that struck her fancy, it would be hers. Maybe Elliott was lying, trying to place the blame for his crime elsewhere. In the distance, a siren wailed. Soon Elliott would be in official custody and Dante would be on his way back to Sara. If Elliott was the man who'd harassed her and killed Maddie Phillips, this job was over. He should be relieved. He wasn't.

When the sirens were close, the wounded man on the ground gave a gurgling laugh. "You shouldn't be sitting here, man. Time's a wastin'. Things didn't go right. Those sirens are a dead giveaway, and as soon as Mama figures out you're not dead, she's gonna take it out on the girl, for sure."

"What the hell are you talking about?"

"Why do you think I didn't just shoot you in the kitchen?" Elliott asked sharply. His hands were bunched into tight fists. "I could've shot you and run and not had to worry about being chased at all. That's what I wanted to do, but Mama wanted you out of the house so she could have some time with Sarabeth, and she figured if I got you away from the house…"

Was Elliott trying to get rid of him so he'd have a chance at escape? In his condition that was unlikely. "Why would Opal want time with Sara?"

"You better quit asking questions and run, hotshot,"

Elliott said hoarsely. "Mama's patience has been wearing mighty thin lately, and trust me when I tell you she never had a whole helluva lot of patience to begin with."

Those were the ramblings of a madman, Dante was sure, but they caused a surge of nausea. He was dizzy as he rose to his feet. "Explain," he snapped. "Fast."

"Mama wants it all," Elliott said as the flashing lights of the ambulance flickered over the park. "Since you've busted me up and ruined Plan A, the only way left is to get rid of the girl, but she's got to get some papers signed first so all the money will come to us when Sarabeth is dead."

Dante nodded to the approaching paramedics and then he turned and ran. As he ran he tried to convince himself that Elliott was lying, trying to take revenge for his ruined knee. Opal wouldn't hurt Sara, no matter what she wanted. And still, his heart lodged in his throat as he kicked up the pace.

The sound of sirens caught Opal's attention, and she grimaced. Then she muttered a foul word Sara had never expected to hear from the usually proper woman.

Of course, the gun was out of character, too.

"That moron," she muttered. "He always manages to screw up everything I ask him to do."

"What moron?" Sara asked softly.

Opal pinned angry eyes on Sara. "Elliott. Give him a simple job and he can't manage to finish it. Ask him to woo a girl and he does everything wrong so she ends up despising him." She scowled. "Ask him to get rid of an interfering pest and he screws that up, too."

Sara didn't have to ask. Dante was the pest. Since

Elliott never would have called for police or an ambulance, Dante had obviously come out on top.

"He'll be home soon," Sara said.

"Home," Opal said with a gentle wave of the gun. "You so easily call this place *home,* when by all rights the house and everything in it should be mine. Mine and Elliott's. We earned it, by blood and by devotion. It's ours. As soon as you sign the papers I've had drawn up, it will be ours legally, as well as morally, and this will all be over."

Unlikely. Sara did not bother to argue with the unbalanced woman. "You should leave while you can. I don't want to see you hurt."

Opal smiled. "You wish it would be that easy, don't you?" She pressed the muzzle of her gun to Sara's forehead. "I'm leaving, but I'm not going alone. You're coming with me."

Dante ran as hard as he could, his feet pounding into the ground. Dogs barked, disturbed by the night's excitement. The moon and the occasional floodlight lit his way.

As he ran he had visions of finding Sara as he'd found Serena. Lifeless, bloody, taken from him by a swift and senseless act of violence. He was too late, always too late. The pictures in his mind were horribly vivid; the memory of the smell of fresh blood filled him, and he ran harder.

The kitchen door of the dark house stood open, just as he'd left it. He ran through the opening, calling Sara's name. Screaming. All the while he told himself that she'd remained in her room as he'd told her to. He replaced the gruesome images in his head with more pleasant memories. Sara lounging on the bed, Sara reaching for him, Sara smiling. She would be there, unaware of her housekeeper's betrayal. Safe. Always safe.

He ran up the stairs, again calling her name. She didn't answer. When he reached the top of the stairs, he saw that the bedroom door was standing open, and his heart stopped. His feet froze.

He could not go in there. He couldn't do it. His flesh crawled, and his heart fell into his stomach and lay there like a brick. A hard, useless brick. His legs seemed ready to go out from under him.

"Sara?" he called her name more softly this time, praying for an answer, praying that she would come walking through that doorway to greet him. For a moment his feet were glued to the floor. He couldn't move. He couldn't breathe.

And then he did, because he couldn't stand there forever, not knowing what was on the other side of that doorway.

The room was empty.

While he was terrified for Sara and what might've happened, he was also relieved. Sara might've gone to a neighbor's house. That was it—she'd run for safety and found it. He snagged his cell phone and opened it, intending to call Hawkins and Potts and get them over here ASAP. He had no signal. He walked to the window. Still no signal. He saw Sara's cell phone and snagged it, flipping it open to find the same message, even though she had a different carrier.

The signal was being blocked, and that showed a level of planning that terrified him.

He searched the house, calling Sara's name, pushing

furniture aside and tearing the place apart. Afraid of what he might find, and just as afraid of finding nothing, he finally ran into the backyard and around to the side, intent on going to a neighbor's house for a freakin' phone.

What he saw there stopped him cold. One pink slipper lay in the side driveway well behind his parked pickup truck. He knew the slipper hadn't been lying there very long. When he'd left the house that slipper had been under Sara's bed. Had she left it there for him on purpose, or had Opal knocked it off forcing Sara into the car? At least he knew Sara wasn't dead, not unless there was someone else involved in this crime. Opal couldn't possibly lift Sara's deadweight.

Since he was almost positive this was a sick mother-and-son operation, without third-party assistance, he felt a rush of relief. Sara was alive. For now.

Opal drove with one hand and kept a firm grip on her gun with the other. The weapon was no longer pointed directly at Sara, but it was there and ready. Opal's hand seemed steady enough, even though she drove much too fast as she sped through the deserted Tillman streets. They were not headed in the direction of the small, neat house Opal shared with her son. If Sara wasn't mistaken, they were headed for the interstate.

And from there...?

If Opal hadn't been driving so fast, Sara would have considered releasing the seat belt the older woman had insisted she wear and jumping from the car, taking her chances. But the seat belt was less than easy to operate, she'd discovered in putting it on, and the landscape flew by much too fast. Sara wore a long pajama top, her summer robe and one slipper. None of these things would offer protection against the asphalt.

Ten minutes after leaving Sara's house, Opal took the ramp that fed her onto the interstate, southbound. Leaving Tillman added a new layer of terror to the ordeal. What if no one ever found her? What if Opal pulled to the side of the road, shot Sara, and dragged her body into the wooded area that lined the interstate?

She'd been alone for a long time, but she'd never felt so completely on her own.

No, she was not alone. In spite of all their problems, Dante would find her. Somehow, someway—and hopefully soon.

A stack of papers sat on the car seat between them. Sara had not signed them, and Opal had not yet shoved them at her and insisted. Was it a will? A power of attorney? How had Opal planned to get what she believed to be hers? It didn't matter now. If Elliott had been caught, the entire plan was ruined.

If the night had gone as planned, no one would've ever known the truth. If Elliott had killed Dante and Opal had gotten her papers signed and then killed Sara, no one would've suspected the housekeeper who had been with the Vance family for all her adult life. How long would she have waited before unearthing the papers that would give her everything? Days? Weeks? Months?

Thank goodness Dante wasn't easy to get rid of.

"Why?" Sara asked simply, wondering if she could judge what might happen next by Opal's motivation.

She didn't have to elaborate. Opal glanced at her, and there was a touch of sadness in the lined face lit by the dash of her reliable midsize car. "Everything that's yours should be mine," Opal said cryptically. "The house, the money, the social standing...everything I was denied. I thought if you married Elliott and he moved into the house and claimed his legal rights, all would be well." She shrugged her shoulders. "Well enough, anyway. I could've moved in after a while, and when there were children the future would be set. But as usual Elliott blew it. He came on too fast and too clumsily, and you made it clear you didn't have any interest in dating him, much less considering marrying him. Then he decided he was in love with Maddie Phillips. That slut. She was married, but she didn't dress or behave like a married woman, and she drew my Elliott into her wicked web."

"I don't understand."

Opal glanced Sara's way. "Have you never noticed the resemblance? Have you never noticed how much Elliott and Robert look like brothers?"

A chill danced down Sara's spine. "They're... brothers?" She saw no resemblance at all between her beloved late husband and Opal's unappealing son.

"Half brothers. They have the same father." Opal's face grew hard. "Shelby Vance did right by me all those years. He arranged my marriage, and no one ever suspected that Elliott wasn't T. L. Greenwood's child. While Shelby was living he gave me and Elliott money. He gave us everything we needed but it was never enough to make up for what he didn't give us. Recognition. Love. The family home that should've been ours."

"You can have the house," Sara said. "I don't even like it all that much."

Opal sneered. "You're lying."

"No, I'm not. I have no fond memories of that house. I never lived there with Robert, I didn't choose the furniture and the pictures myself, it's too big and too empty and I would love to see you and Elliott living there."

"Too late," Opal mumbled. "Much, much too late."

"It's never too late."

Opal's chin came up. "I've killed for what's mine. The money I've embezzled from the estate might've been explained away if you'd discovered it in the midst of all your newfound interest in finances. *That* I could survive, I suppose, but when I killed that Phillips slut, everything changed."

Sara gripped the door handle with one hand and the seat-belt latch with the other, wondering if a jump from the car would kill her. She glanced at the speedometer. Opal was driving 85 miles an hour. "You? You killed Maddie?"

"Yes. What was I supposed to do? The plan was so simple. We just wanted to scare you a little. We were sure you'd turn to us for assistance and comfort. After all, we worked very hard to become your only family." She sighed tiredly. "But that bastard Mangino showed up at the wrong moment, and as it turns out Elliott liked my plan too well."

"Too well?" Sara prompted, glancing at the speedometer and wondering if Opal would ever slow down.

"He got carried away and stole that slut's underwear, before I ever got around to taking yours. Then he left that fancy whore underwear on her porch, too. You were rightly frightened by the anonymous and inappropriate gift. Maddie, on the other hand, was somehow charmed." Opal scoffed in disapproval. "Elliott has disappointed me often during the years, and he did so again. Instead of giving his attention to you, as he should've, whether Mangino was around or not, he kept watching Maddie, waiting to see if she was wearing the underthings he'd left for her."

"Is that why you killed her?" Sara asked, her voice cracking. "Because Elliott wasn't doing as you asked?"

"It was more than that. Maddie saw Elliott the night before she died. She caught him peeking in her window like a common peeping Tom. The girl was this close to figuring out that Elliott was the one. By then I'd already left you the identical replacements he'd purchased in Birmingham, and we couldn't have the two incidents tied together."

Sara shook her head and gripped the doorknob so tightly her hand hurt.

"So much has gone wrong. Tonight has been a disaster, but it all started going wrong long before tonight. You were supposed to turn to me and Elliott for help," Opal said once again. "You were supposed to ask us to move in with you, to comfort you the way family does. It would've turned into a permanent situation, before too long, and in such close quarters you and Elliott were bound to become familiar. The disposable phone I bought was supposed to be entirely untraceable. I checked it out on the Internet, and then I hear that bastard Mangino talking about how close they are to finding out where it was purchased. I couldn't have that."

The woman sighed tiredly. "I thought after a while you'd see through Elliott's flaws and discover the similarities he and Robert share. You would've loved him, eventually." Opal pulled sharply around a semi that was moving too slowly to suit her. "Instead you turned to someone else. You let Dante move into the house. You saw past *his* flaws. You fell in love with the wrong man, Sara."

Elliott folded, spilling his guts about his mama's plan, his biological father and the birthright he'd been denied. All this while under the care of a team of paramedics as they prepared him for a ride to a Huntsville hospital that was well equipped to handle his wound.

Dante didn't think Opal would be foolish enough to take Sara to her home, knowing—or at least suspecting—that her son had been caught. Still, Hawkins and Potts were headed in that direction to verify that they weren't there. After that, they'd be meeting him here, in the park, where blue and red lights flashed and neighbors had gathered to witness the excitement.

Jesse leaned over his prisoner, refusing to allow Dante to get too close. "Where would your mother take Sara in a situation like this one, Elliott?" Jesse's voice was calm, even, the voice of a friend who only wanted to help. "You failed, she's panicking. Where would she go?"

Elliott shook his head. "I don't know."

"Sure you do," Jesse said. "Does she have a relative or a friend she'd turn to in a time like this? A particular place where she might feel safe?"

Elliott shook his head, but even from a distance Dante caught the spark of fear in his eyes.

"The son of a bitch knows something," Dante said sharply. "He's no better a liar than he is a thief." He remained outwardly calm, but inside his heart was pounding too hard and his stomach was filled with butterflies. "If you can't make him tell, I will." He didn't have a gun on him at the moment—Jesse had taken it from him when he'd arrived at the scene of the shooting, after finding Sara gone—but he could get one at a moment's notice. "He's got another knee, after all," he added in a lowered voice.

"Keep him away from me!" Elliott said, jutting a finger in Dante's direction. "He's nuts!"

"I'm nuts?" Dante took a single step closer to the wounded man. "I'd say you and your mama have me beat in the crazy department. Now, tell me where I can find Sara…."

Dante moved one step closer, and Elliott went pale. "She'll kill me if I tell."

Did he really think his own mother would kill him for spilling the beans? It sure looked that way. "I won't kill you," Dante promised. "I'll shoot your other knee, and then I'll start breaking bones. You won't ever walk again by the time I'm through with you—but I won't kill you."

"Dammit, Dante!" Jesse said, spinning around. "You can't do this!"

"I can and I will."

"Daddy's fishing cabin," Elliott whispered. "Mama said if anything went wrong, we could meet up there after."

"Things went wrong, didn't they?" Dante said.

Elliott nodded. "It shouldn't have gotten so messed up. Mama just wants Sara to give us what's rightfully ours."

"Well, I promise I'll do everything I can to make sure you both get what you rightfully deserve," Dante said sincerely.

"Really?" Elliott said brightly, and then he sobered as he realized exactly what Dante might think they deserved.

"Where is this cabin, Elliott?" Dante asked. "Help me out. You're not a murderer." *Like your mother.* No wonder Maddie Phillips hadn't seen danger coming. Who could've imagined a woman like Opal Greenwood pulling a kitchen knife and using it in a violent manner?

Maddie's death was another reason Elliott had told everything. In his own sick way Elliott had loved the young woman. His mother had taken her life.

After a short hesitation Elliott began to give directions to the fishing cabin on Mills Lake. As the man finished and the paramedics closed the ambulance doors, Hawkins and Potts drove into the park.

Reinforcements.

Jesse turned to Dante, surely knowing what he planned. "Give me fifteen minutes to call the sheriff and get a team together…."

Fifteen minutes. No way in hell was he waiting that long. "You can meet us there," Dante called as he ran toward the rumbling car where Hawkins and Potts waited. He couldn't be sure that Sara had an extra fifteen minutes…and he wouldn't lose another one. Not tonight.

Chapter 12

They'd been off the interstate for at least ten minutes, driving toward the lake, according to the signs they sped past. Sara had visions of being shot and dumped in the water. No one would hear a gunshot out here, so far from civilization, and if they did hear anything the noise would be so distant they wouldn't give it another thought. Now that they were off the interstate, Opal was driving much slower. Sara continued to grip the door handle and the seat-belt latch, waiting for the right moment. Opal didn't seem to think her prisoner would attempt escape. Sara had been quiet and downright meek for the past several miles.

Did Opal still want her papers signed? Was she trying to figure some way out of this mess or was disposing of her problem—namely Sara—all that was on her mind at the moment? Either way, Sara knew the woman who held her captive didn't intend to allow her to see another sunrise.

When Opal turned the car onto a narrow dirt lane, she had to slow the car considerably, and that's when Sara made her move. Without any warning she released the seat belt and threw open the car door. With a minimum of maneuvering, she threw herself out, bumping her shoulder on the car door and hitting the ground hard. Opal screamed, and then she fired her weapon. Sara waited for the sting of a gunshot, as she rolled away from the car and into the tall weeds that lined the dirt road.

Her body had been badly jarred when she'd hit the ground, and her shoulder hurt where it had banged into the car door, but other than that she felt no pain. She had not been shot. She'd made it. For now.

Sara didn't stand up to run but stayed low and crawled as quickly as she could away from the narrow dirt road and the car. She tried not to think of snakes and coyotes and whatever other wild animals might be lurking in the same tall weeds that protected her. She thought only of Opal's gun and the fact that the woman she had relied on for years had already committed murder and would not hesitate to do so again.

She'd started this journey with one slipper on, since she'd purposely kicked off the mate as Opal had forced her into the car. The other had flown off as she'd jumped from the car, so her bare feet scraped along the ground. Her toes already felt raw, but that didn't slow her down.

Dante would see that slipper she'd left in the driveway beside her house and realize what had happened, she knew. Somehow he would find her, even though

Opal had driven into a dark and quiet wilderness. Sara was barefoot and wearing only a pajama top and a thin robe as she scraped and scrambled through the tall weeds. Her arms and legs were already scratched and she ached everywhere from the jump from the car, but she didn't dare stand up. No, she scrambled like a wild animal escaping from a hunter.

Opal called her name. The angry woman screamed, and Sara was very thankful that the sound did not seem to be very close. It was so dark that Opal could likely not see the movement of the weeds that were disturbed by Sara's escape. After one call and one scream, all was silent but for the whishing and cackling sounds of Sara's low flight.

After a while she stopped to listen. Her heartbeat was rapid and hard, her breathing harsh, so much so she was worried that Opal would hear. She hadn't heard the car pull off, but she'd been so intent on getting away she hadn't been paying close enough attention to the noises beyond her own circle. She knew she had to be making noise, even though she tried not to, so it might be best to be still for a while. To sit and wait. If Opal thought her prisoner had escaped, maybe she'd make a run for it.

Maybe.

Sara knew from what she'd seen during the drive that she was very close to the eastern edge of Mills Lake. Her papa had brought her here to fish more times than she could count, so she knew the area well. In just a few hours there would be fishermen on that lake, some in boats and others on the bank. If she could just remain hidden until then, she'd be all right. She'd be able to get help as soon as the sun rose.

She pressed her forehead into the earth and took a deep breath. She smelled dirt and rain and the musty scent of decaying leaves. Her heart pounded against her chest and, it seemed, against the ground she clutched. She'd been lying there very still for a few minutes before she realized that her entire body was shaking. She closed her eyes and thought of Dante. If anyone could find her, it would be him. In the middle of the woods, in the middle of nowhere…he could find her.

But would he find her in time?

Dante allowed Potts to drive only because the man had been behind the wheel when he'd pulled up to the park and Dante didn't want to take the time to do something so simple as change drivers. As they sped down the interstate, he checked the weapon Hawkins had provided.

Opal Greenwood was not their usual opponent. She was a matronly older woman who'd cooked for him, who'd kept Sara's house, who went to church every Sunday and doted on her only son. She knitted and made quilts in her spare time, and she was an active member of the Tillman Beautification Society. She made tea and cookies.

She'd also murdered Maddie Phillips—if Elliott could be believed—and she'd kidnapped Sara and tried to have him killed just to get him out of the way. Appearances could be deceiving. No joke.

Dante worked at narrowing his focus so he didn't worry to the point of distraction. He did his best to make this just another rescue, just another job he was being well paid to handle.

The problem was, Murphy's words were coming back to haunt him. *She's it.* Sara was it for Dante, and he'd known it all along. She was the one woman in the world who was different from all the rest. Different for him, only for him, in a scary soul-deep way. When she'd asked him to stay, he should have said yes. He should have changed his life for her. Given another chance...

No one said a word until they were within minutes of the cabin Elliott had directed them to.

"Plan?" Hawkins said simply.

"We find them, we separate them so Sara's no longer in danger. Take the old woman alive, if you can," Dante said evenly, "but Sara is the priority."

"No question about that," Potts said, as they made a turn and found themselves staring at the rear end of a parked car, headlights still on and driver's-side and passenger-side doors both standing wide-open. Tall weeds and inky black surrounded the car, but he did spot one fluffy pink slipper lying beside the passenger door. He could easily imagine what had happened, and for the first time in days he smiled. "Good girl."

Sara crawled slowly forward, trying not to make any noise and at the same time doing her best to put as much distance between her and Opal as was possible. Her knees and elbows were raw, and something small but pesky had stung her ankle. A twig had scraped across her cheek and its passage had stung as much as the bite to the ankle, but she didn't make a sound. She thought of a warm bath and a big glass of sweet iced tea and Dante's arms. Nothing else mattered. Nothing.

When she hadn't heard any sounds of pursuit for a while, she bravely lifted her head and looked around. In the near distance there was a small cabin, windows dark, no car in the driveway. The idea of hiding indoors was appealing, but this cabin sat at the end of the road Opal had taken, so it could very well be her final destination for the night. The woman could be waiting there, hiding in the dark herself.

No, hiding in the tall grasses for a while longer would work just fine, thank you very much.

Sara lay on her back in the obscuring weeds and looked up to the dark night sky, listening for Opal's approach—or the disturbance of low grasses by reptilian creatures. She heard neither. There was not even a moon to light the night, since clouds had come rolling in, and while that made her passage more difficult, it was also a blessing. If it was hard for her to see, then it was just as hard for Opal.

Her heart was hammering and she was scared out of her wits, so to keep from panicking she turned her thoughts to Dante. She'd thought she had all the time in the world to convince him that they had something special. He was naturally reluctant where their relationship was concerned. Not physically, but emotionally he definitely held back. He was determined to keep a distance and remain his own man, to avoid the ties of family and love and commitment. Still, she was sure he loved her, and she certainly loved him.

She should have left town with him when he'd asked her to. She should have trusted her heart to lead her, instead of turning to her head for guidance.

Why did she continue to hang on to whatever it was

that she and Dante had? Now that she'd reclaimed her life, now that she'd proved to herself that she could and should love again, Sara knew that she wanted more than great sex and a few laughs from the man she loved. She wanted forever and babies and the promise that he would never leave her. She wanted comfort and excitement, dancing and laughing, trust and commitment.

Most of all, she wanted him to *find* her!

She hadn't been lying there long when she heard the even, rhythmic rustle of the tall weeds that offered her cover. Sara held her breath and lay very still. Sweat covered her trembling body in spite of the coolness of the night, as what were surely footfalls came closer. Closer and closer. Her heart pounded. She didn't want Opal to come across her this way, flat on her back and defenseless. The idea of facing the woman and her gun again was terrifying, but she'd run before and if she needed to run again in order to survive, she would.

Sara rolled onto her side and eased up to peek over the top of the high grasses and weeds. Her eyes had adjusted to the darkness, and she saw the figure coming her way. All she could see was a shadow, the vague silhouette of a person. Opal was not giving up quite as easily as Sara had hoped.

The dark figure stopped. Had she heard Sara breathing or moving? Did she hear the pounding heartbeat? Before Sara had the chance to dip back down a flashlight beam hit her in the face.

She didn't hesitate but popped to her feet and ran toward the cabin. Maybe there was a phone in there, or a door she could get behind and lock. Swerving to one side and then to the next to make herself a less attractive target, and hoping with all her heart that Opal was a lousy shot, Sara waited for the loud pop of a gunshot. Instead, what she heard was a sharp cry of her name in a deep, familiar male voice.

Sara stopped running so quickly she stumbled and almost fell again. She spun around and now, even in the darkness, she recognized Dante's form and face.

He didn't slow down but ran into her and wrapped his arms around her, lifting her from her feet. "Where's Opal?" he asked, his voice unusually hoarse.

"I don't know," she said. "When the car slowed down, I jumped out and I ran. I didn't look back."

"That's good," he whispered.

Her heart continued to pound and breathing was difficult. "I know she was chasing me, at least for a while, but I haven't heard her for the past few minutes. Maybe she gave up and left."

"The car's still here."

Even though Dante was holding her, Sara felt a new rush of fear. "Then so is Opal."

Dante snagged a two-way radio from his belt and informed whoever was on the other end that he had Sara and she was safe. A voice—Hawkins's—responded that they would continue to sweep for the old woman until the sheriff arrived and took over.

And Sara held on to Dante, her own personal lifesaver, her guardian in so many ways. He had found her, just as she'd known he would.

The first order of business should have been to find and restrain Opal. But Sara was shivering and her face had been scratched. She was halfway dressed and her usually neat hair was tangled and adorned with dried grasses and twigs. He was not leaving her alone, not in the cabin, not in the car, and sure as hell not out here in the dead of night. Hawkins and Potts could keep looking for the nasty old lady who had killed Maddie Phillips and terrorized Sara. Besides, there was something he had to do.

"You're it," he said softly.

Terrified and clinging to him, she still managed to laugh. "What is this, Dante, some sick game of tag?"

"Not that kind of *it*."

"Oh." She settled more snugly against him. "That's good, huh?"

"I haven't decided yet," he said honestly. This was going to turn his life upside down. Living was so much easier when you didn't have anything to lose. Now suddenly he had everything to lose, and he didn't like that at all. And at the same time…he did.

"You're it, too," she said, calming down considerably. "For me, you're definitely *it*. I knew you would find me. I knew it without a doubt. I love you, Dante."

He kissed her because she was right in front of him and he could. It should have been quick, something fast and easy to seal the deal before he moved on to find Opal. Instead, there was passion and promise in the kiss. There was relief and bonding in his mouth against hers. She was his, and he wasn't going anywhere. Not without her.

"Jesse will be here soon, with the sheriff and a crew of deputies," he said. "I'm going to carry you back to the car and we'll wait there for the reinforcements to arrive. Then I'll take you home."

"You don't have to carry me," she said.

"You've got no shoes," he said, hanging his flashlight from his belt, there beside the walkie-talkie and then lifting Sara off her feet with one arm—whether she liked it or not—and tossing her over his shoulder. He scanned the area, taking in his surroundings, finding no immediate threat. Sara might have been more comfortable in another position, but he wasn't about to holster his gun in the name of anyone's safety—not even Sara's.

"I'd hate to see how you'd carry me if I wasn't it."

"If you weren't it, you'd have to walk."

"I offered to walk," she countered.

"We can't have that." He caught the gleam of what might be broken glass straight ahead. A breeze caught the hem of Sara's bathrobe and flipped it up. "No underwear," he said casually as the bathrobe fell back into place.

"The evenings have been warm lately, so I've been sleeping in little or nothing. If you'd come to my room more often in the past few days, you'd know that."

"My mistake, I can see that now," he said softly. "Still, this is no way for the mayor to leave the house."

"Strangely enough, Opal did not give me the opportunity to dress properly before she kidnapped me." There was a hint of friendly sarcasm in her voice.

"I told you not to open the bedroom door to anyone but me."

Sara sighed. "I was trying to get to a phone. Opal had some cell-phone blocker thingie."

"A thingie."

"Yes. I'm sure you know a more technical term, but whatever you call it, it should be against the law."

"I'm pretty sure it is." The banter was easy, now that

he held her, now that he'd confessed that she was it, for him. In the distance, sirens blared. Soon the law would be here and his job would be done. No, his job would have just begun. Talk about scary stuff. "Do you still want kids?"

"That's a pretty abrupt change of subject," Sara said, squirming.

"Well, do you?"

"Yes, but…"

"I suppose we should get married first, you being the mayor and all. We can't have a scandal right out of the gate."

Her body stiffened. "Did you say *married?*"

"Yep." Somehow he'd thought she'd be pleased, but she didn't sound all that thrilled.

"You can't propose to a woman in the middle of a crisis, while she's hanging half-naked over your shoulder and unable to even look you in the eye! My hair is a mess, I have on no makeup… I'm not prepared!"

"Why not? You said you love me. I love you. The rest is just formalities, right? No preparation necessary."

"This is so wrong," she said lowly.

"What's so wrong?"

"You've never said that you love me before this, and now that you do I'm… I'm…"

"I know. Half-naked and unable to look me in the eye. Ratty hair, no mascara, unprepared…"

"There's a proper way to do such things, you know."

"You're way too hung up on what's proper, Madame Mayor." Even though she had not yet said yes, she would. Sooner rather than later, he imagined.

"Well, somebody has to…"

Sara didn't get to finish, because the woman who had kidnapped her stepped out of the shadows into the beams of her car's headlights—beams that had created deep shadows on the fringes in which she'd hidden. Opal aimed her weapon to the side, more toward Sara than him, and ordered Dante to drop his gun.

He did, and since he was quickly unarmed and was still carrying Sara over one shoulder, Opal relaxed. Dante took a step forward, moving toward the older woman. Older and a woman, yes, but no less deadly than any other murderer. She thought she had him at a disadvantage, but she was wrong.

"Sloppy work, Mr. Mangino," Opal said with a superior air in her voice. "Your cohorts are on the opposite side of the field, and you're so busy wooing Sara and her money you apparently didn't even think to keep an eye out for me."

He didn't bother to argue that he didn't care anything about Sara's money. Anyone who would go to such lengths to have it for herself wouldn't believe him, anyway. "What do you want? Make it quick, you old battle-ax. You can hear the sirens as well as I can. They're coming for you." He took another step toward her.

"I don't suppose what I want matters much anymore," Opal said sadly. "But I won't go gently, Mr. Mangino. If I can't have what is rightfully mine, then she won't have it, either."

There was no more time. Help was still too far away, and Opal was on the verge of breaking. "Sorry, honey," he said as he dropped Sara to the ground and surged forward, using one well-placed swift kick to disarm Opal. Her weapon went flying and fell into the tall weeds that had concealed Sara. When that was done, he spun around and kicked her legs out from under her. She dropped to the ground hard, with a surprised cry.

Beside him Sara was righting herself and her robe while uttering an indignant "ow" or two. Eyes on Opal, who was breathless and harmless at the moment, Dante offered Sara a hand. She took it and rose to her feet.

Instead of chastising him for throwing her to the ground, she said, "Nice work."

"You okay?"

She leaned into him. "I'm sore all over and a woman I loved like family tried to kill me. *Okay* is probably not the right word for the moment." She hung on to his arm. "But I'm gonna be okay very soon," she said gently, and he understood.

With a word into the radio, Potts and Hawkins came rushing back to the car. They took custody of Opal, for the time being, so Dante could give all of his attention to Sara. They didn't talk about the fact that everything had changed. There was no more talk of the future and what it might bring. He just held her, and she held him.

When Jesse and the sheriff arrived, Dante allowed Sara to make one brief statement, and then he snagged the keys to Potts's car and took her away. Before they reached the ramp to the interstate, she pointed to a dark country road that led into darkness.

"I think that's the road I'm looking for. Turn here," she instructed.

He did.

Chapter 13

"There's a boatload of deputies just down the street," Dante said gently. "Sure you want to take this chance?"

"Positive. They're much too busy to bother with us, at the moment. Besides, I can't wait. I'm a fully grown woman, patient and cautious and usually proper, and I can't wait until we get back to my house before I have you inside me again."

Her words had an effect on him. He moaned a little, and pushed his hand up her pajama top to caress her breasts. His body swayed over hers, and then he lowered his head to kiss her.

They were parked at the end of a dead-end road, surrounded by ancient tall trees. A short walk away the water of the lake lapped, and when sunup came, there might be a few boatless fishermen parked here. But for now, no one else was near.

All was dark and warm and electrifying and safe, in the backseat of this borrowed car. Their sweating bodies were entangled. They were as frantic and full of heat as they had been eighteen years ago.

But everything was different, now. It was better. There was hope and love, as well as passion. "Say it again," she said as she took her mouth from his and wrapped her legs around him.

"You're it," he said. "You're the one." He pulled roughly at her pajama top and buttons went flying. The fabric fell back, leaving her exposed. "I love you," he finished.

"I love you, too," she said breathlessly. "I think I always have."

"Are you sure about this?" he asked.

"Yes," she whispered. "Are you?"

He kissed her throat and aroused her with his fingers until she was ready to shatter. That was his answer, and she relished it. The sensations he created in her were wonderful, but she didn't want this to be over, not yet. She danced on the edge and she liked it there. This was paradise. This was what she had waited a lifetime for.

She unfastened and unzipped his jeans, lowered them over his hips, and took him in her hand, stroking and guiding, touching the tip of his erection to her. He barely entered, and then he withdrew, and then he teased her again and she gasped as she gripped his hips and insisted that he fill her.

He did. Again and again, until she couldn't think of anything but the way he felt inside her and the way he loved her and the promise he was making to her at this moment, when he kept nothing from her. Nothing at all.

She shattered, clutching him to her and holding on for life and heart and love. She gasped, she cried out and something within her broke.

She was free. Wonderfully, totally free. Loving Dante liberated her. She was not afraid, not of life, not of love, not of making a mistake.

Dante came hard, burying himself deep inside her and practically growling her name. Depleted, he lay atop her and took a few ragged breaths, and she wondered if he felt as wonderfully free as she did. Had he finally let go of the past?

The windows were fogged up, they were tangled and sweaty, and Dante's legs were too long for the back-seat. Sara laughed. "Okay, we can go home now."

"That means I have to move," he said.

"Sad but true." She touched the side of his face. "The payoff for our sacrifice will be a hot shower and a soft mattress. That's something to consider."

"You talked me into it."

The drive home was too long, but the silence that stretched between him and Sara was comfortable and easy. She was safe. He was in her life for good, it seemed. Just a few days ago that very thought had struck fear into the pit of his soul, but now the idea of sticking together forever seemed like the right thing to do. For her and for him, it was right.

Dante couldn't help but wonder if Sara was already pregnant. Unlikely, he imagined, but the possibility filled his mind. He had fought the very idea of fatherhood for so long, but coming close to losing Sara had broken down his defenses and he found himself dreaming of things he'd never wanted before. Would he regret all he'd said and done come morning? When the excitement was over, would he write off his surrender to fear and relief?

He imagined a little girl with dark blond hair running down the stairs of that stuffy old house, bringing life and laughter to ancient walls, filling a space in his heart and his life that he hadn't even known was empty. He imagined a little boy playing T-ball with Jesse's kids. No, he would have no regrets.

He would do his best to keep Sara and whatever family they had safe, but in reality he knew eternal safety was impossible. Living meant taking chances. True happiness meant he'd have something to lose. Every day was all the more precious because life was uncertain.

Back at the house, he and Sara thoroughly enjoyed the hot shower and the soft mattress. He lost himself with her and inside her. He didn't know how many times he told her he loved her, or how many times she spoke the words herself. They laughed, in spite of the horror of the evening, and he doctored her thankfully minor wounds.

They slept, wrapped in crisp white sheets and one another's arms. When he woke well past sunrise he spread her thighs and buried himself inside her and made her come one more time. She gave everything she had to him, without reservation. She shattered beneath him, and moments later she slept once more.

He wanted to stay here in this bed forever, without the complications of reality, but that wasn't possible. A man could only hide for so long. Too soon Dante left the bed, dressed, and wrote Sara a quick note. Before she woke again, he was gone.

* * *

Sara was sore all over, but she was also deliriously happy. Betrayed, shocked, battered...and loved. The love more than made up for the rest. She'd expected to find Dante in the bed with her, but he was not. The house was quiet. Too quiet. She reached into her closet and pulled out a winter robe much too heavy for a warm spring morning. Her summer robe had been ruined last night.

Tying the belt as she walked down the stairs, she called Dante's name. There was no answer to her call. For the first time, she felt a ripple of unease. She was safe, so in spite of everything he'd said and done last night, did he consider himself done? How could he say he loved her and then bolt?

When she smelled the coffee she relaxed a little. A man who was bolting in terror didn't stop to make coffee.

She didn't find Dante in the kitchen, but he hadn't been gone long. The coffee was still hot. Since the machine automatically cut off after two hours and it was still operating, she knew he hadn't left hours ago. He'd stepped out, that's all. When she saw the note that was rolled up and stuck in her pink coffee mug, which had been placed beside the coffeepot, she knew she'd find an explanation there.

The note made her heart leap.

Stuff to do. Back in a few days. Don't call. Love you. Dante.

Stuff? A few *days? Don't call?* Her heart eased at the "Love you," but still... Stuff to do?

She sighed and poured herself a cup of coffee. He'd be back. He wouldn't have said so if he hadn't meant it. And if he'd asked her not to call, then he had a good reason. She loved and trusted him with everything she had.

Maybe a few days on her own wouldn't be a bad thing. She had a few things to take care of herself.

Dante really, really hated cemeteries. He hadn't been to this particular Georgia cemetery in six years.

Serena Loomis, Loving Daughter and Good Friend.

He knelt and placed a small bouquet of mixed flowers at the base of the headstone. "Sorry I didn't come by sooner," he said softly, as if there was anyone else around to hear. "Time got away from me, I guess."

Why lie to a headstone? There was no one here but him and maybe something of Serena. "Hell, the truth is I was scared to come here. I didn't want to face you because I had failed so miserably and because I never got up the nerve to tell you that I loved you. I did. I would've done anything to save you, but I wasn't given that chance." He squirmed, wondering if he should have put on a suit and tie for this excursion. No, Serena wouldn't care. She'd fallen in love with him, thinking he was a janitor whose idea of dressing up for a special occasion was changing T-shirts. "Anyway, believe it or not, I'm actually going to be getting married and maybe having kids, if it all works out like it's supposed to and our parts are all in good working order." He could very well imagine Serena laughing at him right now. The wind rushed through the trees, and for a moment he thought he actually heard her.

"I love Sara, but that doesn't mean I didn't love you.

I hate that what happened to you happened, but that doesn't mean I'm not supposed to live."

Another gust of wind came out of nowhere, and it felt as if something warm brushed his cheek. "You'd like Sara," he said. "She's a lot like you, and at the same time...not like you at all. You could be friends, if you ever met." Then he laughed. "I sound like a woman, don't I? I definitely sound like a wuss. Don't tell anybody." He glanced around the cemetery, which suddenly seemed more peaceful than ominous. "Wish me luck. I hope wherever you are you're at peace."

There was only one more thing to be done. In the short time they'd been together, Serena had often chastised Dante for choosing limericks as his poetry of choice. But she'd laughed even as she'd censured. She'd laughed a lot. "I'm not sure I even remember how to do this," he said. "But here goes. There once was a man from Paducah..."

A short while later he stood, brushing the grass and dirt from his knees. He'd said what he'd come here to say, and then some, and he had a feeling he wouldn't be dreaming about Serena anymore.

In a few hours he had crossed the state line and was back in Tillman, anxious to see Sara. He'd been gone five days. Getting everything accomplished had taken a little bit longer than he'd planned, but it was finally done. Maybe he should have called her, but he'd known if he heard her voice, he'd tell her everything and then there would be no surprise. He wanted to surprise her. He wanted Sara to know that he would gladly change his life for her. Besides, he didn't need to call. He'd told her he'd be back. That was enough.

He'd been prepared not to answer Sara's phone calls if she didn't follow his directions, wondering at the same time if he could do that, if he could see her number on the caller ID and not answer. She hadn't called, not once, so he'd never know if he would have passed the test or not.

He had one stop to make before he went home. Jesse wasn't in the office but had left a large, bulging manila envelope with Dante's name on it. Dante grabbed the envelope and headed for the house that was becoming home, the house where he could so vividly see his life stretching before him. He would settle down in one place, for Sara. He would become the man she wanted him to be.

The first thing he saw when he pulled onto her street was the large, bright orange For Sale sign in front of her house.

"Oh, hell, I knew I should've called," he said as he pulled to the curb. She had probably thought he wasn't coming back. Maybe the house held too many bad memories for her, thanks to Opal and Elliott, but they had made some good memories there, too. Hadn't they? Were they enough? He grabbed the manila envelope and ran toward the front door.

"Sara!" he called as he walked through the front door. Once again, she had not set the security alarm.

She stepped out of the parlor, and for a moment he held his breath. She wore jeans that fit her just so and a T-shirt that hugged her breasts. She wore flip-flops with sparkly things on them, and her hair was pulled up in a ponytail. Her smile was real and relaxed. "It's about time," she said, as if she had never doubted him.

He jerked a thumb toward the front of the house. "What's with the For Sale sign?"

"I made a few changes while you were gone," she said as she walked toward him.

"What kind of changes, other than the ones I can see with my own eyes?" he asked, only slightly suspicious.

"I resigned my position as mayor. I never wanted the job anyway, and the vice-mayor is more qualified than I ever was." She wrapped her arms around his neck. "I signed legal papers making Owen responsible for all the Caldwell charities and I hired a lawyer to see to the Vance financials." She rose up on her toes and kissed him. "You missed the shoe burning."

"There was a shoe burning?"

"Anything that pinched my toes was toasted, and I donated all my suits to a charity that helps to clothe women who are just getting out into the business world."

"Interesting," he breathed.

"So, ask me," she whispered.

"Ask you what?"

"Ask me one more time," she said, her voice low and enticing in a way that spoke to his body. He was so easy where she was concerned.

"Marry me?"

Sara sighed. "Fine. Be stubborn. Pretend you don't know what I'm talking about. I'll ask you." She pressed her body to his. "Run away with me, Dante Mangino. Let's get in your truck and go where the wind takes us. As long as we're together, nothing else matters. Nothing."

He laughed, and she backed away. It was obviously not the response she was expecting.

Dante opened the manila envelope with his name on

it. Inside there were papers making his employment official, along with a badge that would mark him as a Tillman investigator. She peeked inside, and after a moment of surprise she, too, laughed.

"I quit my job with Bennings," he said, "and I put my house down south up for sale. I called Jesse and told him he owed me a favor. A big one. When I told him what I wanted, he didn't seem to mind."

"Of course he didn't mind," Sara said with love. "You're the most fabulous police officer this city has ever seen. He'd be a fool not to take you back. So, what happens now?" she asked, seemingly unconcerned at their less-than-solid state of affairs.

Dante dropped the manila envelope and its contents to the foyer floor. He kissed her and then he lifted her off her feet. "We can have whatever we want. For now, for today…run away with me?"

Sara wrapped her legs around him and held on tight. "Yes, please."

And the world was theirs.

Epilogue

Five years later

Running away from everything and everyone had been a blast, for about a year. He and Sara had gone to an island in the Caribbean for a couple of months, and then they'd come back to Alabama for Murphy's wedding. The marriage of the Benning Agency's geek and Cal's sister had been traditional. There were tuxes and champagne and tons of bridesmaids, and the bride had been a vision in white.

Dante considered Sara a much more beautiful bride, in red, and when they'd said their vows there hadn't been a tuxedo in sight.

After the wedding they'd spent some quiet time at a mountain park out West. Money wasn't a problem. She had plenty and so did he. They saw the places they wanted to see and did the things they wanted to do. They made up for lost time.

In that first year Dante had taken on the occasional short job for Bennings, when he felt like it and the agency was in dire straits, but the guys all knew, as he did, that he was finished with that life. Sara had taken dance classes. Jazz, ballet, ballroom dance classes she insisted he participate in. All of it had just been for fun, and she'd reveled in it. He'd reveled in watching her, in seeing her so happy.

Then she'd gotten pregnant. Apparently, everything in the reproduction department really did work as it should. Maybe too well, since they ended up with not one kid but two right out of the gate. Dante was pretty sure the twins had been conceived after one of the dance classes Sara had dragged him to. The tango.

In the end they'd had to settle down somewhere, and they'd found their way back to Tillman. Sara had sworn off politics, and Dante was glad of it, but she was delighted to be close to her good friends Patty and Lydia again. The sock burning that first year had been a real doozy.

Jesse had tried to entice Dante into coming to work for the city, but Dante was no cop and he knew it. He was best at training. He'd known it all along. So that was what he did. He trained. The Mangino School for Martial Arts did a booming business. Students came from as far away as Huntsville, and the Tuesday-night ladies' self-defense class was always a hoot—and always filled to capacity. Sara liked to say, "Woe be to any purse snatcher who foolishly makes his way to Tillman, Alabama."

Dante hadn't done any more than trim his hair in five years, so it was long once again. As usual, he wore it pulled back for class. Since his hair wasn't thinning or going gray, at least not yet, he figured he was allowed. Besides, Sara liked it long. She liked it a lot. Hell, he'd shave his head if he thought it would turn her on.

His students for this particular class stood in motionless and well-trained formation, eyes straight ahead, shoulders back. They were prepared for anything; they were fearless; they were his favorite class.

They were all three and four years old. His best students, his own Beth and Jack, stood front and center.

Sara watched from her usual seat at the side of the room, where the other mothers and fathers sat to observe the class. They watched but were not allowed to interfere. It was one of his rules, and so far no one had questioned it—or any other rule. Sara said he could look intimidating and even scary when he wanted to, but even his fiercest glare made Beth and Jack giggle.

He gave them that fierce glare now, and Beth pressed her lips together to contain her laughter.

His wife loved him, and he loved her.

His kids adored him, and he couldn't imagine life without them.

His mom was a much better grandmother than she'd been a mother—and she didn't visit too often.

Life was good. Dante was home, now and forever, and all was well with the world they had built.

* * * * *

THOROUGHBRED LEGACY
*The stakes are high when it comes to love,
horse racing, family secrets
and broken promises.*

*A new exciting Harlequin
continuity series coming soon!*
Led by New York Times *bestselling author
Elizabeth Bevarly*
FLIRTING WITH TROUBLE

Here's a preview!

THE DOOR CLOSED behind them, throwing them into darkness and leaving them utterly alone. And the next thing Daniel knew, he heard himself saying, "Marnie, I'm sorry about the way things turned out in Del Mar."

She said nothing at first, only strode across the room and stared out the window beside him. Although he couldn't see her well in the darkness—he still hadn't switched on a light...but then, neither had she—he imagined her expression was a little preoccupied, a little anxious, a little confused.

Finally, very softly, she said, "Are you?"

He nodded, then, worried she wouldn't be able to see the gesture, added, "Yeah. I am. I should have said goodbye to you."

"Yes, you should have."

Actually, he thought, there were a lot of things he

should have done in Del Mar. He'd had *a lot* riding on the Pacific Classic, and even more on his entry, Little Joe, but after meeting Marnie, the Pacific Classic had been the last thing on Daniel's mind. His loss at Del Mar had pretty much ended his career before it had even begun, and he'd had to start all over again, rebuilding from nothing.

He simply had not then and did not now have room in his life for a woman as potent as Marnie Roberts. He was a horseman first and foremost. From the time he was a schoolboy, he'd known what he wanted to do with his life—be the best possible trainer he could be.

He had to make sure Marnie understood—and he understood, too—why things had ended the way they had eight years ago. He just wished he could find the words to do that. Hell, he wished he could find the *thoughts* to do that.

"You made me forget things, Marnie, things that I really needed to remember. And that scared the hell out of me. Little Joe should have won the Classic. He was by far the best horse entered in that race. But I didn't give him the attention he needed and deserved that week, because all I could think about was you. Hell, when I woke up that morning all I wanted to do was lie there and look at you, and then wake you up and make love to you again. If I hadn't left when I did—the way I did—I might still be lying there in that bed with you, thinking about nothing else."

"And would that be so terrible?" she asked.

"Of course not," he told her. "But that wasn't why I was in Del Mar," he repeated. "I was in Del Mar to win a race. That was my job. And my work was the most important thing to me."

She said nothing for a moment, only studied his face in the darkness as if looking for the answer to a very important question. Finally she asked, "And what's the most important thing to you now, Daniel?"

Wasn't the answer to that obvious? "My work," he answered automatically.

She nodded slowly. "Of course," she said softly. "That is, after all, what you do best."

Her comment, too, puzzled him. She made it sound as if being good at what he did was a bad thing.

She bit her lip thoughtfully, her eyes fixed on his, glimmering in the scant moonlight that was filtering through the window. And damned if Daniel didn't find himself wanting to pull her into his arms and kiss her. But as much as it might have felt as if no time had passed since Del Mar, there were eight years between now and then. And eight years was a long time in the best of circumstances. For Daniel and Marnie, it was virtually a lifetime.

So Daniel turned and started for the door, then halted. He couldn't just walk away and leave things as they were, unsettled. He'd done that eight years ago and regretted it.

"It *was* good to see you again, Marnie," he said softly. And since he was being honest, he added, "I hope we see each other again."

She didn't say anything in response, only stood silhouetted against the window with her arms wrapped around her in a way that made him wonder whether she was doing it because she was cold, or if she just needed something—someone—to hold on to. In either case, Daniel understood. There was an emptiness clinging to him that he suspected would be there for a long time.

* * * * *

THOROUGHBRED LEGACY
coming soon wherever books are sold!

Cole's Red-Hot Pursuit

Cole Westmoreland is a man who gets what he
wants. And he wants independent and sultry
Patrina Forman! She resists him—until a Montana
blizzard traps them together. For three delicious
nights, Cole indulges Patrina with his brand of
seduction. When the sun comes out, Cole and
Patrina are left to wonder—will this be the end of
the passion that storms between them?

Look for

COLE'S RED-HOT PURSUIT

by USA TODAY bestselling author

BRENDA JACKSON

Available in June 2008 wherever you buy books.

Always Powerful, Passionate and Provocative.

REQUEST YOUR FREE BOOKS!

2 FREE NOVELS PLUS 2 FREE GIFTS!

Silhouette® Romantic

SUSPENSE

Sparked by Danger, Fueled by Passion!

YES! Please send me 2 FREE Silhouette® Romantic Suspense novels and my 2 FREE gifts (gifts are worth about $10). After receiving them, if I don't wish to receive any more books, I can return the shipping statement marked "cancel." If I don't cancel, I will receive 4 brand-new novels every month and be billed just $4.24 per book in the U.S. or $4.99 per book in Canada, plus 25¢ shipping and handling per book plus applicable taxes, if any*. That's a savings of at least 15% off the cover price! I understand that accepting the 2 free books and gifts places me under no obligation to buy anything. I can always return a shipment and cancel at any time. Even if I never buy another book from Silhouette, the two free books and gifts are mine to keep forever.

240 SDN EEX6 340 SDN EEYJ

Name	(PLEASE PRINT)
Address	Apt. #
City	State/Prov.	Zip/Postal Code

Signature (if under 18, a parent or guardian must sign)

Mail to the **Silhouette Reader Service:**

IN U.S.A.: P.O. Box 1867, Buffalo, NY 14240-1867
IN CANADA: P.O. Box 609, Fort Erie, Ontario L2A 5X3

Not valid to current subscribers of Silhouette Romantic Suspense books.

Want to try two free books from another line?
Call 1-800-873-8635 or visit www.morefreebooks.com.

* Terms and prices subject to change without notice. N.Y. residents add applicable sales tax. Canadian residents will be charged applicable provincial taxes and GST. This offer is limited to one order per household. All orders subject to approval. Credit or debit balances in a customer's account(s) may be offset by any other outstanding balance owed by or to the customer. Please allow 4 to 6 weeks for delivery. Offer available while quantities last.

Your Privacy: Silhouette is committed to protecting your privacy. Our Privacy Policy is available online at www.eHarlequin.com or upon request from the Reader Service. From time to time we make our lists of customers available to reputable third parties who may have a product or service of interest to you. If you would prefer we not share your name and address, please check here. ☐

SRS08

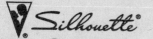
Romantic
SUSPENSE

COMING NEXT MONTH

#1515 PROTECTING HIS WITNESS—Marie Ferrarella
Cavanaugh Justice
Having left medicine, Krystle Maller is shocked to find a man lying
unconscious on her doorstep. She's been in hiding from the mob since
witnessing a murder. She fears her discovery might get her—or him—
killed, yet she treats her handsome patient. While a gunshot wound may
slow him down, undercover cop Zack McIntyre is skilled at protecting the
innocent. And he certainly won't let Krystle handle a dangerous threat on
her own....

#1516 KILLER TEMPTATION—Nina Bruhns
Seduction Summer
Finding a dead man at the start of her dream job is Zoe Conrad's worst
nightmare. But when the man proves to be very much alive—plus
charming, filthy rich and sexy as all get out—Zoe knows she's in even
more trouble. Giving in to Sean Guthrie's incendiary seduction could be
her worst mistake yet. Because while Sean claims to know nothing about
the serial killer who's stalking couples on the beach, local authorities have
their eyes on Sean and Zoe...and so might a murderer.

#1517 SAFE WITH A STRANGER—Linda Conrad
The Safekeepers
On the run with nowhere to hide, Clare Chandler would stop at nothing to
protect her child. Army Ranger Josh Ryan has spent his life hiding from
his true identity and relates to the way Clare keeps herself guarded when
he rescues her and her son from her ex's henchmen. In order to help them,
however, he must face his family and the truth of who he really is...while
withstanding his fiery attraction to Clare.

#1518 DANGEROUS TO THE TOUCH—Jill Sorenson
Homicide detective Marc Cruz doesn't care for second-rate con artists—
especially those claiming they have psychic powers and a lead on his
serial-killer case. Although Marc intends to expose Sidney Morrow for the
hoax she is, her impressions—about the investigation and his attraction to
her—are proving all too true.

SRSCNM0508